Harmony

Holly J. Martin

ISBN: 0692977686
ISBN-13: 9780692977682

To my mother
You always said I was in love with love,
and you were right!
I love you.

David Johnson   Elsie Johnson

Marcus

Henry

Theodore (Teddy)

Mason (Bear)

Garrett

Bobby & Ty

Davey

Caleb

Jack

1

MacKenzie danced around her tiny Upper East Side loft apartment smiling and reading the headlines from the *New York Post:* "Tears in Harmony as renowned pastry chef dies." It was so wrong on so many levels to be this happy about the passing of a fellow human being, but she couldn't help herself. This was exactly the break she had been waiting for since she moved to New York six months ago. Six long months of making thousands of cupcakes in her friend's shop in SoHo. How different her life had looked a year ago, she mused. Back then she was living in the most beautiful city in the world, Venice, Italy. She was in a committed relationship with a man she loved, and she held a position as a fledgling pastry chef in the most prestigious restaurant in all Italy.

MacKenzie walked to the window of her tiny apartment, looked down at the busy morning commuters, and sighed. Look at me now, she thought with a wan smile: single and probably staying that way, with a quirky sense of humor, working at a cupcake shop (albeit the hottest cupcake shop in SoHo), living in the tiniest apartment she had ever seen. MacKenzie shook her head, held up the paper again, and resumed her dance around the loft, holding the paper like her waltz partner. Not today. She wasn't going to let anything get her down today, she thought as she waltzed to the tiny bathroom to shower and get ready for the day on which she intended to dazzle Davey Johnson.

She felt good walking down Fifth Avenue holding the binder carrying her freshly printed-out resume. A smile tugged at her naturally red lips. She still hadn't gotten used to the lightness of her head since she cut her lion-size mane of red curls when she moved to New York. A fresh start, she had told herself when she made the appointment at the trendy Manhattan salon. She had left hardly recognizing herself, with shoulder-length, loose waves and a new lease on life. She felt like Mary Tyler Moore, and if she had been wearing a beret, which she actually did own, she would have tossed it high into the air and twirled, she was so happy. She let the smile drop and tried to look serious as she pushed through the gold doors of Harmony.

"Hi, lunch for one?" the pleasant hostess asked MacKenzie.

MacKenzie shook her head. "Um, no, actually, I came to drop off my resume for pastry chef and please, please don't think ill of me for dropping it off so soon after the passing of Monsieur Lastat, but I know the restaurant business and know that things happen very quickly. Kind of the show must go on, you know?" she replied apologetically.

The hostess nodded, took the binder, and smiled sweetly. "You're absolutely right. Monsieur Lastat will be missed greatly, but his position must be filled, and you are hardly the first to send your resume along. I will make sure the manager receives it."

MacKenzie stared at the young hostess blankly. "Is there something else?" the hostess asked.

MacKenzie shook her head and smiled. "No, no, thank you. Have a lovely day!" she blurted as she bolted out of the restaurant.

Red faced, MacKenzie walked toward the subway. Face palm. Stupid. What had she thought? That Davey Johnson, master chef and owner of the hottest restaurant in Manhattan, would be standing there taking resumes and offer her the job straightaway? Sipping her coffee contemplatively as she rode the subway into SoHo Village, MacKenzie tried to come up with a sensible answer for any interview question regarding her present employment. It was like once being the CEO of a huge company and having to explain to someone why you were now a barista at Starbucks. *Ugh*.

MacKenzie smiled as she walked into Sweet Love, the cupcake shop where she presently worked. Her sweet friend and fellow baker Charlotte lumbered over to greet her. "Hey, there, girlfriend!" Charlotte exclaimed, leaning on the counter with a smile. "Has that hunky Dave Johnson stolen you from me yet?" She asked it with a twinkle in her eye.

Charlotte was the sweetest person ever, as far as MacKenzie was concerned. Too sweet for the competitive pastry chef business. Charlotte and MacKenzie had been roommates for the year they attended the exclusive Gastronomicom Culinary School in France. From Dublin, Ireland, the curvy, dark-haired, dark-eyed, beautiful Charlotte had immediately earned her friendship when she wore a T-shirt to the campus orientation the first day that read "Screw Mr. Darcy, I'm waiting for Jamie Fraser." MacKenzie had walked right up to her and claimed her as her partner in crime, and they had been thick as thieves ever since.

Charlotte was not great under pressure and hated the cutthroat culinary world. After they graduated, Charlotte had come to New York and opened a small cupcake shop that had grown to be the hippest place in New York to get your sweet fix on.

MacKenzie couldn't have been happier for Charlotte. Especially since, in the last year, Charlotte had managed to snag a millionaire husband with a ginormous sweet tooth—hence the fateful meeting and falling in love of the two in the cupcake shop while he was getting his sugar fix. She had gotten pregnant, which was why, when MacKenzie was literally crying to her on the phone about her breakup and wrecked life, Charlotte had asked MacKenzie to take over the shop until something else in the restaurant business came along. Charlotte's new husband didn't want her working the long hours and having to manage the stress of running the business while she was pregnant. MacKenzie was happy to help her friend, but more importantly, it gave her the much-needed focus on anything other than her own life. And it helped her afford food and lodging, albeit sparse. At least her father, the General, hadn't had to be called, thought MacKenzie, and she smiled.

"Hi there, my sweet Irish lassie. How are you feeling besides tired and pregnant?" MacKenzie said, hugging her friend from behind.

"Bloody big as a house is how I'm feeling and jealous of your cute skinny jeans and heels," Charlotte replied, smiling.

"Well, I'm here now, so you can go home to rest. Megan will be here shortly to help out. I dropped off my resume, and my fingers are crossed," MacKenzie said, holding up her crossed fingers.

Charlotte slapped one of her hands. "Only cross one, lass! Don't you know that crossing both hands is bad luck?" she said laughing.

MacKenzie giggled. Charlotte was the most superstitious person she had ever met. She loved that about Charlotte, considering her own up-bringing with the staunch outward appearance of the General. Although at home the General was not strict or uptight but the most loving and sweet father any girl could ask for.

She missed him and her mother. They were still living in Harmony, Maine, and had every intention of retiring there and never relocating again. She must call the parentals tonight and tell them of the new de-velopments. MacKenzie knew her parents couldn't understand why she didn't just march into Davey's restaurant and ask him for a job. Her parents loved all the Johnsons and felt sure that Davey would have helped MacKenzie out, but that was not how she wanted to get a job. She had some pride, and besides, her resume was impressive on its own.

MacKenzie gave herself a mental shake and then ushered Charlotte out the back door to the town car that was waiting to take her home. She waved goodbye and settled in to make some cupcakes.

2

avey leaned back in his office chair, closed his eyes, and sighed. What a shitshow this week had been. His friend, who worked at his restaurant and happened to be the best pastry chef in New York, had died unexpectedly; a woman he had dated twice had burst into his restaurant last night trying to cause a scene, screaming at him, asking him why he hadn't called her; and he and his brothers had finally located Jack, his sister, but they couldn't seem to get through to her because of her PR people. Another sigh. Shit. Davey jumped up, grabbed his duffel bag, and headed to the bathroom. A run was what he needed. A nice long run with his music blaring in his ears and only his thoughts to keep him company.

As he walked out through the lobby area of the restaurant, Mike, his manager, hollered to him. Davey stopped and stared at Mike. Mike was a tall British black man with impeccable taste in suits who considered himself something of a player with the ladies. In spite of this, or maybe because of it, he was the best restaurant manager in the business. He was sharp and professional. Davey liked that. "What's up? I'm going for a run. I'll be back before the evening prep," Davey announced, putting in his earbuds.

Mike was holding out a stack of folders. Davey put up his hands. "If those are what I think they are, then you handle them. Set up what we talked about, and I will let you know who to call in to interview after I taste their dessert. Pick no more than five from the stack, and make sure they can come in next week while I'm not traveling."

Mike smiled. "Sure thing, chief. Have a good run," he replied.

Davey gave him the thumbs up and switched on his music. Aah, a warm spring afternoon, Creedence blaring "Proud Mary" in his ears. Davey just let the sidewalk swallow him up.

Freshly showered and feeling better than he had in days, Davey stood in the crow's nest, an office overlooking the restaurant, surveying the activity below. A soft tap on the door brought him to attention. "Come in," he said, not moving from his stance at the one-way glass walls of the crow's nest. Bobby, Ty, and Marcus strolled in, looking like they were up to no good. Davey smiled. "Look what the cat dragged in," he said, giving each of his brothers a man hug.

"Bro! What's up?" Bobby asked, coming to stand at the window to peruse any attractive females on the floor.

Marcus took a seat. "I heard about your pastry chef. Sorry, man," Marcus said.

Davey shrugged. "Thanks. I got to know him a little while he was here, as much as you can know an old French chef set in his ways and speaking very little English, but he was the very best at what he did, and it certainly leaves a hole in my staff. We're going to start the hiring process this week."

Ty went to stand beside Bobby, checking out the dining room. "I hear you had a disgruntled lady calling you out last night," he smirked, nudging Bobby, his twin.

"Jesus, news travels fast, but I'm not surprised. I was having a drink at the bar with Caleb when she started going off," Davey said, shaking his head. Caleb, the next to the youngest Johnson sibling, had a habit of stirring the pot whenever he could.

"That is exactly why I don't date anyone beyond two dates. It starts to get messy after two dates," Davey said, going to the fridge, pulling out beers, and passing them around. "So what's on the agenda for tonight?" he asked his brothers.

They all shrugged. "No plans. I know a little pub that Jared usually stops in for a beer a few blocks away. You want me to call him, and we can meet there for a while?" Bobby asked.

Davey nodded, finishing his beer. "Sure, sounds like a plan. Let's get out of here."

After three games of darts and many shots later, the brothers and Jared sat at the bar reminiscing about all the times they had buried the four-wheelers in waist-deep mudholes during the summers at camp. The guys all had their backs to the bar except Caleb, who had met them there with Jared. He leaned back with his elbows resting on the bar, surveying the room. Eventually, a blonde sashayed up to the bar and stood in front of Caleb. The cute blonde grabbed the front of Caleb's flannel shirt to steady herself, as she was clearly drunk. "Hi, there. Do I know you?" she slurred. Caleb smiled.

"Hi, beautiful. If we had met, I would surely have remembered," he said, letting her lean on him.

She giggled. "You're cute. What's your name?" she asked, starting to list.

Caleb caught her just as a very large man came from the back and spied the blonde seemingly being embraced by Caleb. The man stalked toward them, looking like he wanted to kill someone. "What the fuck is going on here?" the very large man said.

Caleb held up his hands in surrender but quickly caught the blonde again as she started to lean over. He chuckled. "Hey, man, she just came over to say hi. She thought she knew me, but we have not had the pleasure yet."

The man glowered at him.

The blonde giggled again. "You're such a gentleman," she said, looking up at Caleb with adoring eyes.

The man pulled the blonde away from Caleb, sat her in the nearest chair, walked back over to Caleb, and got in his face. "You think you're cute, don't you, boy?" the man growled.

Caleb put his elbows back on the bar and leaned back as if he didn't have a care in the world. "Let me see. I do believe you're asking a rhetorical question, but if not, then the answer is yes. I have it on good authority that I am indeed cute. Don't you guys think I'm cute?" Caleb asked, addressing his brothers and Jared.

They all chuckled, and Marcus mumbled, "Fucking adorable."

Caleb's smile got wider. "See, I told you," he said to the pissed-off man in his face.

The man grabbed Caleb by the shirt. "Well, I say you come outside with me and show me how fucking adorable you are," he said, starting to pull Caleb away from the bar.

A strong hand grabbed the man's wrists and held them in place. "Let. Go." Davey ordered, turning his head to the man in Caleb's face.

The man looked at Davey. "Who the fuck are you, his boyfriend?" he growled.

Davey looked the man straight in the eye. "No, motherfucker, we're his brothers, and unless you want your ass kicked three ways to Sunday, you better fucking let him go. Nobody gets to mark up that pretty face except us. Now fucking beat it," he said calmly.

The man looked at Davey and then at Marcus, Bobby, Ty, and Jared before he slowly let go of Caleb's shirt, grabbed his girl, and walked out the door. Smiling, Caleb downed his beer, turned around, and ordered shots all around.

— ⁓

Davey woke to pounding in his head. Jesus. Why did he let his brothers goad him into so many shots? he wondered as he got up, took some pain relievers, and guzzled some water. He grabbed his phone on his way back to his bed. He hadn't felt this shitty in a long time, but he still smiled as he thought of his brothers and Jared stumbling out of the bar when it closed and serenading the city with Frank Sinatra's "New York, New York" as they walked the few blocks home. Bobby, Ty, and Jared shared a cab to their apartments, and Marcus and Caleb crashed at his.

Davey dialed his manager, Mike, as he lay back down.

"Hey, chief, what's up?" Mike answered.

"Hey, buddy, I'm not going to be in this morning, and I have afternoon meetings. I will be in this evening. My dad is in town, so I am having dinner with him tonight around seven," Davey whispered as quietly as possible in order not to wake his brothers.

"Well, that could be a problem, chief. I have the first applicant coming in to make dessert this afternoon. I thought you wanted to meet them," Mike said.

Davey groaned. Shit. "Well, it can't be helped. I will still be in for dinner and have some of the dessert. If it is good enough, I will have them come in for an interview with me next week. Call the Corner Market and set it up for the applicants to grab whatever baking supplies they need. Gotta go. I'll see you tonight," he said, hanging up his cell phone, burying his head beneath the pillows, and groaning.

3

The old-fashioned rotary phone ringtone rang over and over before MacKenzie's hand blindly found the phone and held it to her head. "Hello," she croaked.

"Is this MacKenzie O'Riley?" the British male voice asked.

MacKenzie sat bolt upright with a hand to her pounding head. "Yes, it is," she said, trying to sound alert and professional.

"Splendid. Splendid. This is Mike Austin from Harmony, the restaurant you recently submitted your resume to for pastry chef. I know this is short notice, but I will need you to come in today and make a dessert for this evening. If you come in early enough, you can get your supplies at the Corner Market up the block. Can I expect you within the next two hours?" he asked.

"Oh my! Yes, of course, I will be there. Thank you so much!" MacKenzie said, completely forgetting about her headache.

"Excellent. See you then."

The phone went dead. MacKenzie flopped back down on her bed, trying to get her bearings. "OK, OK. Think, think. You can do this. Just get up and take some pain medication and hop in the shower. You will feel better after a shower," she said as she slowly got up from the bed before running to the toilet to lose whatever was left in her stomach from the night before. Ugh.

What had she been thinking when the crew from Ink had come over and insisted she join them next door in the crazy, dirty drinking game of Scrabble? MacKenzie harrumphed as she climbed in the shower. Fun. That's what she had been thinking, and God, it had been so much fun. The crew from the tattoo parlor next door to the cupcake shop appeared to be rough and dangerous, but really, they were very sweet people who had befriended her not long after she took over the cupcake shop, and boy, did they love their cupcakes! The crew and customers of the tattoo parlor made up probably a fourth of the weekly revenue.

Initially she had thought it was funny that, as the game began, everyone took a shot of Jack, and then more shots followed no matter whose turn it was. It was really just dirty Scrabble, meaning you could only use dirty words, and while you were thinking, you drank a lot. MacKenzie washed her hair and laughed, remembering some of the nasty words that had been used in the game. Some of them she needed to google to find out the meaning when she had a chance.

Dressed in her black slacks, a white button-down blouse, and black heels with her hair pulled back in a proper bun, MacKenzie squared her shoulders and headed out the door to find a greasy breakfast sandwich to eat on the way to the restaurant. For some reason, and there surely must be medical data to back this up, whenever she imbibed too much, if she ate a greasy breakfast sandwich the next day, she felt better. Maybe it was all in her head, but it worked.

Walking into the diner, MacKenzie found a seat at the bar and ordered coffee, black, and a cheese, bacon, and egg sandwich. Ed, the kind old cook, spotted MacKenzie on the bar stool, lifted the order ticket, and laughed. "Are you feeling poorly today, Mac?" he asked, holding up the ticket and smiling.

MacKenzie looked up from her coffee cup and smiled weakly. "The greasier the better please, Ed," she replied sheepishly.

Ed nodded. "You got it, sweet pea," he said and got to work.

MacKenzie frequented the diner often. It was just easier than cooking and eating by herself. She had gotten to know most of the waitstaff and Ed the cook while she had been in New York. She enjoyed their stories of crazy customers and often bounced baking ideas off them. Ed's best advice to date was just KISS—keep it simple, stupid. It really applied to all of life, including baking.

She downed the sandwich and coffee and hollered to Ed, "Wish me luck!" and made for the door.

Everyone at the counter hollered "Luck!" and Ed hollered "You got this, sweet pea!" Even though she hadn't even told them what the luck was for, she felt like they were all rooting for her. New Yorkers. Who said they weren't friendly?

MacKenzie felt a little better, but nerves were making her already-sensitive stomach flip-flop as she walked through the doors to Harmony. It was deserted, but MacKenzie could hear talking and pans clattering toward the back. MacKenzie followed the noises and opened the doors that led to the giant kitchen. A large scary-looking man in an apron was talking with a well-dressed African American man when MacKenzie opened the door. They both looked up and just stared for a moment. The African American man had a moment of remembrance and walked toward her with his hand outstretched. "Hello, you must be MacKenzie. I'm Mike Austin, the manager here at Harmony. I was the one who called you," he said.

MacKenzie smiled and shook his hand as she gazed around the kitchen for any signs of Davey. "Yes. It's nice to meet you," she said, looking at Mike's hand that still held hers as he continued to stare at her.

"Oops, sorry," he said, releasing her hand. "Well, Mr. Johnson is not here this morning and has meetings in the city this afternoon, but we do things a little differently here anyway. Each applicant is going to prepare the evening dessert of their choice based on the special meal of the day. When you have decided, you can go to the Corner Market up the block and purchase what you need. Mr. Johnson will try each and every dessert for one week, and based on what he likes and what the customers order, the applicant who makes the best dessert will be offered the position as pastry chef."

The back of the cooking kitchen was another cooking galley set up specifically for desserts and baking. Pure heaven. All stainless-steel appliances and a very large granite island. MacKenzie inspected the stoves and opened the large stainless-steel fridge to see what ingredients were stocked. MacKenzie's fingers got the familiar need to express herself through baking. When she directed her gaze back to Mike, she found him watching her with amused interest. "What is the meal special today?" she asked calmly.

Mike nodded his head. "Well, no pressure, but today is a special day. Mr. Johnson's father is in town, and the Johnsons are from Maine, so we are serving Maine lobster and corn on the cob.

MacKenzie smiled. David Johnson is in town. Hmm, I think I know just what to make and still follow the golden rule of KISS, she thought.

"Well, OK, then. I will be off and let you get to it. If you need anything, I will be working in my office out back," Mike said, pointing to a door down the hallway.

"OK, great, and one more thing: How many on average does Harmony serve on Monday evenings?" MacKenzie asked.

Mike smiled. "Good question. On Monday, we serve approximately three hundred customers," he said and turned toward his office.

OK, so realistically, not even half those people would have dessert, but just to be on the safe side, we'll go with one hundred fifty dessert plates. MacKenzie was doing the math in her head when she laughed. It so didn't seem fair, but she just happened to know what the owner's father's favorite dessert was because she had made it for him numerous times, and it went perfectly with tonight's meal. So not fair, MacKenzie thought, but I will take this as a sign straight from God and run with it. She started making an inventory of what she would need to purchase at the Corner Market.

MacKenzie's hand was starting to cramp up from peeling all the apples she needed to make her Maine apple crisp. All she had needed to purchase from the market were apples and grated mild cheddar cheese, her secret ingredient. MacKenzie had found that the freezer was full of Gifford's French vanilla ice cream for à la mode. She was not surprised to find Davey supporting a Maine grassroots ice cream company by serving its products in his restaurant. Even better that they had the best moose tracks ice cream on the planet. One of the many, many things she missed about Maine.

After the crumble was added to the top of the crisps, she popped them into the ovens to bake. The stoves were very similar to the top-of-the-line ovens she had used in culinary school in France. On the big chalkboard in the kitchen, MacKenzie wrote "Maine apple crisp à la mode" and took a deep breath.

By midafternoon, MacKenzie was finished. She walked back to Mike's office and knocked. "Come in," Mike said.

MacKenzie walked in and stood in the middle of the room in front of his desk. "I'm all done. I'm assuming you don't want me to hang around to serve tonight," she said, folding her apron.

Mike shook his head. "No, we will have the wait staff serve tonight, but if you're hired, you will be expected to be here for the bulk of the evening to attend to the desserts and perhaps make fresh coffee and such," he said.

MacKenzie nodded. "Of course. Everything is cooled and in the walk-in cooler. It will just need to be put in the warming oven at approximately five o'clock and I left a note for the temperature of the oven and the ice cream is in the freezer, of course," she said nervously.

Mike got up, walked to her, and held out his arm. "Nice work. If it tastes as good as it smells...well, you can guess," he said smiling. "I will walk you out." He gestured for her to walk ahead of him.

On her way to Sweet Love, MacKenzie tried to focus on the ingredients she would need for this afternoon's cupcakes, but she kept going back to second-guessing herself about what she had selected for dessert. Was it too simple? Would the other pastry chefs outshine her with extravagant desserts? This went on until she reached the cupcake shop. It was busy, and she rushed in, washed her hands, and threw her apron on.

Charlotte mouthed "Thank you" as she started bringing fresh trays of cupcakes out to the display case.

When the rush was over, MacKenzie told Charlotte what had happened at Harmony and about her doubts about her dessert selection. "Bollocks is what I say!" Charlotte exclaimed. MacKenzie laughed and leaned on the counter. "I say it was bloody brilliant. But putting that aside, would you say that Davey Johnson or his father are pretentious?"

MacKenzie shook her head. "God, no! David Johnson is a down-to-earth, hardworking Mainer, and his son...well, he is just perfect in every way," she said with a dreamy expression on her face.

Charlotte laughed. "Oh, I say bollocks to that as well. There are none perfect, but there are a few that come vera, vera close," she said, gently rubbing her round belly. "Well, I think you chose well, and you did the best you could. That is all you can expect from yourself. Although you may have been firing from more cylinders if you hadn't spent half the bloody night next door playing dirty charades." Charlotte took off her apron with a smirk.

"Ah, it was dirty drinking Scrabble, thank you very much," Mackenzie corrected her.

"Well, I will say it again—I hate you for your skinny body and your dirty drinking games," Charlotte said as she kissed MacKenzie's cheek.

MacKenzie laughed. "You do not hate me and every pound and every sober night is worth it," she said to Charlotte's back as she left out the back door. Then she sighed and set out her ingredients for the night.

It was late when MacKenzie had made the last of the cupcakes for the next day. That was what she got for spending the morning playing in the fabulous pastry kitchen at Harmony. MacKenzie locked up the shop and headed toward the subway. She couldn't remember a time in the recent past that she had longed for her bed as much as she did tonight.

4

avey was at his desk working when Mike came in to tell him that his dad was there and had been seated. He locked up his desk and headed out to meet his dad. On his way to the table, several customers addressed him and told him how much they loved the restaurant and that the meal was to die for, especially the dessert. Davey smiled, remembering that the dessert had been made by the first of the applicants. He wished he had been around to meet the pastry chef as he had planned to, but he would make sure to see how his dad liked the dessert. David Johnson wasn't much for desserts—more a meat and potatoes kind of guy—so it would be very telling indeed to see what his father thought.

Davey greeted his dad, and David stood to give his son a big bear hug. Davey wasn't a small guy by any stretch of the imagination. At six feet, two inches, he had a lean, muscular body, but he still seemed dwarfed by his hulking six-foot-five-inch father. They sat down, and David took a pull off his Maine Shipyard beer and held up the bottle.

"I'm glad you stock Maine local brews," David said.

The waitress brought Davey the same beer, which was what he usually drank at the bar, and he took a long pull. "Nothing but the best," he said, clinking bottles with his dad.

"So, how have you been, son?" David asked, looking concerned.

Davey set his beer bottle down. "Me? I'm fine, Dad. Why do you look concerned? Things are great. We have a four-month waiting list for dinner reservations, and I will have the pastry chef job filled by the end of this week. All good." Davey laid his hands out in front of him, palms up.

David harrumphed. "There's more to life than business, son, and you're looking kind of rough around the edges. But I do appreciate you stepping up for your brother last night," he said, digging into the salad and fresh bread that were delivered to the table.

Davey shook his head. "Jesus. It's like the old-fashioned phone tree in this family. Is there nothing that gets by you?" Immediately, he regretted his words. He knew that David felt like he had lost his little girl because of his inattention to household matters.

David nodded. "Yup, there is plenty I've missed through the years, but I've also learned a few things as well. And one thing I've always known is that life is meant to be shared with someone special. I know that you feel like you never want to settle down with one woman because you think losing your mother destroyed me, and make no mistake about it, it absolutely did destroy me. But I would do it all over again for the time I did have with your momma. It was worth it, son. I don't want to get too heavy on you, but I really want you to try and let someone past your walls. I promise you, all of life will be sweeter."

Davey smiled. "I promise to give it some thought, Dad," he replied, thinking that there was no way in hell he would ever want to suffer the way his father had suffered since losing the love of his life. Whoever said it was better to have loved and lost than never to have loved at all was full of shit.

The lobster dinner arrived, and they feasted in silence.

The smell of warm apple crisp with French vanilla ice cream wafted David's nose. David moaned and picked up his spoon. Davey smiled; he liked pleasing his father with something so simple. David's first spoonful had him moaning and closing his eyes.

Davey took a bite and was surprised at the brown-sugary goodness with a hint of something he couldn't name that made it delicious. "This reminds me of Mac's apple crisp. I would get her to make it for me whenever she came over," he laughed. Both men scraped their dessert plates clean, something Davey almost never did; he was not as big on desserts as his father was. Davey motioned Mike over to the table. "Can you get me the resume of this applicant?" Davey asked.

Mike smiled. "I have it for you right here, chief." He handed Davey the folder and went to check on the front of the restaurant. Davey opened the folder and just stared at the resume.

"What's wrong, son?" David asked.

"You're not going to friggin' believe this, Dad, but MacKenzie is the pastry chef, and her resume is the most impressive one I have ever seen without years of experience to back it up. "Wow, Davey said, shaking his head and looking up at David.

"Our Mac?" David asked incredulously.

Davey smiled. "Yeah, our Mac." He read over the impressive resume again.

David took a sip of his coffee. "Boy, what a little spitfire that one is," he said laughing. "The General and I have breakfast quite often at the diner when we're home at the same time. Did you know that Mac had the General searching for Jack right from the get-go? She never let up on the search, and the General was actually very helpful in a lot of matters concerning broadening the search. Mac was very distraught about Jack disappearing, so the General let her test out of her last year of high school and got her into a fancy French culinary school. The day before she was leaving for France, the General said she burst through his office doors as he was having a state department briefing with top heads of state and the president of the United States on speakerphone. The General said it was the cutest damn thing he'd ever seen. Mac curtsied and apologized for the interruption but demanded an update briefing on his search for our princess. He said the president laughed and agreed to give the General and Mac some time to talk. The General said Mac took Jack's disappearance very hard. I hope Jack reconnects with her someday. They were good for each other," David said quietly.

Davey closed the folder. "Well, I will have her come in this week for a proper interview," he said.

David stood. "No, son, you will offer her the position. You said yourself that she was qualified, and she is practically part of our family. We take care of our own. And besides, I have it on good authority that she is pretty easy on the eyes." David smiled and gave Davey a big hug goodbye.

5

rina leaned over the counter conspiratorially. "Come on, Mac, just come to the club once with me. You won't have to do anything you don't want to. I promise," she said winking.

MacKenzie narrowed her eyes suspiciously. Trina was an amazing artist and tattooist from next door. She totally looked the part with jet-black Joan Jett spiky hair, lots of black eyeliner, and a smoking hot body covered with tattoos. Mac loved her philosophical debates with the rocker chick, but they always seemed to come back around to Trina wanting Mac to come with her to some new bondage club that had opened recently. "What I really want to know, Trina, is what is it about me that makes you think I would enjoy this type of date? And I use the term *date* very loosely, I assure you," MacKenzie said, smiling mischievously.

Trina laughed and pointed at her as a customer came into the cupcake shop. "Ha! See! I know you're close to giving in and coming with me," she said, laughing as she walked out the door. MacKenzie shook her head. God, never! But the thought of a man completely taking over in the bedroom held her interest, she had to admit. It had been way too long since she had been intimate with a man. MacKenzie felt a pang of sadness as she thought of Roberto. Why had he made her love him and then betrayed her? Men. Ugh!

MacKenzie was on her way home on the subway when her cell phone rang. She didn't recognize the number. "Hola," she answered.

"Hello? Is this MacKenzie O'Riley?" a voice asked.

MacKenzie snapped to attention immediately. She knew that voice. She heard that voice in her secret dreams and had for years. "Um, yes, yes, it is," she said nervously.

"Hi, MacKenzie, this is Dave Johnson, Jack's brother. Do you remember me?" he asked.

MacKenzie felt like her heart had stopped. Did she remember him? She had been in love with him since she was seventeen, for the love of God! "Of course I do," she said laughing.

"Good. How are you?" Davey asked.

"I'm good, really good, aside from hoping to land an interview with the owner of the hottest restaurant in Manhattan," she said.

Davey laughed. "Yeah, that's why I'm calling, actually. Can you come in this evening for an interview? We can have dinner and catch up and interview at the same time. How does that sound?"

"That would be fine," MacKenzie said.

"Great. Then I will see you at seven?"

"Seven it is." Mac hung up and did a little dance around the pole she was holding in the subway car.

MacKenzie opted for a simple tan wraparound dress with nude heels and a beautiful emerald-green cashmere shawl gracefully draped over one shoulder. Her hair was surprisingly easy to style after she'd had it cut to her shoulders in a soft wavy bob. She looked in the mirror and sighed. Her cheeks were pink from nerves and her eyes brighter blue than usual. Her lips were so red anyone would swear she was wearing bright red lipstick. It's just nerves, MacKenzie told herself. Just breathe, and don't pass out and make a complete ass of yourself, or arse, as Charlotte would say.

The restaurant was crowded as she walked through the doors. The hostess remembered her dropping off her resume and must have been alerted that she was interviewing tonight. She smiled warmly. "You must be MacKenzie. Right this way," she said, leading her toward the back of the restaurant.

MacKenzie spotted Davey immediately, and as if on cue, he looked up from the table. Their eyes locked as she continued to the table. Holy hell, how could he have gotten more gorgeous in the last three years? His dark brown hair was short and combed to the side with just enough curl still in it to be a little disheveled looking, making her want to run her hands through it. His intense brown eyes held hers as she made her way to the table.

She smiled when they reached the table. "Hi, Davey," she said in her raspy voice. She seemed to be holding her breath, waiting for him to respond.

Instead, he just stared at her for another minute before he jumped up and held her shoulders as her regarded her. "Jesus, I'm sorry. My God, you're all grown up! I mean, you look much different from the last time I saw you. Oh, I'm just going to shut my mouth now. It's so good to see you, MacKenzie," he said, hugging her. The feel of his hard body along with his musky aftershave had MacKenzie's heart rate increasing and an influx of heat pooling in her nether regions. Just breathe and do not pass out, she repeated to herself.

When they pulled apart, her shawl fell from her shoulder; she took it off and folded it as she sat down. It is way too warm in here, she thought. Before she sat down, she couldn't help but notice Davey's eyes take in the formfitting wrap dress, and he swallowed hard. Nice. It only lasted a moment, however, and then the heat that she had seen in his eyes was gone, replaced with a genuine smile.

Davey held up a bottle of wine, still smiling. "This is not how I usually conduct interviews, although maybe I should consider it, but this is hardly your usual interview. Besides, the job is yours. Your choice of apple crisp was spot-on, and you had my father's eyes rolling to the back of his head. We'll go over the details on Monday, your first day of work," he said.

MacKenzie smiled brightly. "Excellent," she said, clinking her glass with his. "To working together," she said warmly.

"To working together. Now let's catch up. Tell me what you have been up to for the last three years," Davey said, not able to look away from the bluest eyes he had ever seen.

MacKenzie felt like the years had just lifted away and Jack was going to bound in any minute with the other eight Johnson boys. Davey was incredibly easy to talk to, and two hours just flew by. MacKenzie was very careful to stay on point with her school and work history, and she just prayed he wouldn't ask her how she went from a fledgling pastry chef at the most exclusive restaurant in Italy, La Pergola, to Sweet Love cupcake shop in SoHo.

When they had finished the bottle of wine and MacKenzie tried to stifle a yawn, Davey smiled and nodded. "Well, I can see you're tired, especially if you got up to make the cupcakes today, so I will wrap this up. Monday's meal will be smoked salmon for your preparation purposes. You can always shop at the Corner Market for your supplies. You can come in at whatever time you need to start preparing, and I would ask that you stay until the dinner rush is over, usually between nine and ten. Is that OK with you? We will go over everything else Monday at some point," he said, standing.

Mackenzie nodded. She grabbed her purse and wrap and stood up. She swayed a little as she stood, and Davey embraced her arms to steady her. It was like a bolt of electricity went through her. "Oh! Sorry. I think the wine went straight to my tired brain. I'm fine now, really," she said, turning to walk away.

Davey kept his hand on the small of her back as he walked her to the outside doors. "I'm sure you are fine, but for my own peace of mind, I would like to walk you out and put you in a cab. So please just humor me," he said softly next to her ear.

MacKenzie looked at him and caught her breath. She nodded and tossed the wrap over the opposite shoulder. Davey hailed a cab and saw her into it. As she drove away looking at him on the sidewalk with his hands in his slacks pockets, she took a ragged breath and leaned her head back in the seat. Holy shit.

6

oly shit. Davey watched MacKenzie walk to the table. He couldn't take his eyes off her. She was the most beautiful woman he had ever seen. Not the plastic-model kind of beauty but a grab-you-by-the-throat-and-take-your-breath-away-and-make-you-forget-you're-simply-sitting-there-with-your-mouth-hanging-open-like-an-idiot kind of beauty. She was so regal and elegant as she gracefully walked to the table. Her former mane of fiery red hair had been pared down to a gorgeous, shoulder-length bob that was sexily pushed behind one ear; the other side hung down framing her face. Her cheeks were pink like she had been exerting herself, and her lips, Jesus, her perfect red lips were almost impossible to look away from until he looked at her eyes. My God, he had never seen such naturally dramatic almond-shaped blue eyes shaded by impossibly long lashes. Breathtakingly beautiful. When he finally got his wits about him and stood and embraced her, he was immediately under her spell again. With her soft body pressed against him and the light flowery fragrance she wore, he felt his manhood come to life immediately, which could get very embarrassing for both of them if he didn't get a fucking grip soon.

Davey hadn't thought he had made up his mind about the pastry chef position even though his father had put his two cents worth in, but he found the words "The job is yours" just flowing easily out of his mouth. What. The. Hell. If he didn't get a grip, he was going to friggin' propose marriage to her right here at the table.

Oh, there, that helped. He needed to categorize this as exactly what it was, lust. Albeit the strongest surge he had ever experienced but lust, plain and simple. Once he acknowledged it for what it was, he was able to settle down and thoroughly enjoy MacKenzie's company as she told him about all the places she had lived with her parents and her schooling in France and then her internship at the exclusive La Pergola in Venice, Italy. It was such a refreshing change to sit and listen to her stories. He could relate to most of her experiences because he had had similar ones in his culinary schooling. She was a joy to listen to, and as the evening and the wine wore on, she became more expressive, which he found so friggin' adorable.

Before he knew it, the wine was gone, and MacKenzie was trying to stifle a yawn. He felt a pang of disappointment. He didn't want the night to end. What the hell did that mean? No way was he going to fuck his sister's best friend, not to mention his new employee. He had a strict "no dating coworkers" policy for himself personally, and he strongly discouraged it for his staff. No, he would get her a cab and see her on Monday for work. He would be much better prepared on Monday, and this spell he seemed to be under would be gone. Right? That is what he would do, he thought as he closed the door to the cab and stared into the deepest blue eyes he had ever seen.

7

MacKenzie had spent the weekend at Sweet Love, training the new cupcake baker and showing him around the shop. Charlotte was in good hands, which was a load off MacKenzie's mind. Sunday afternoon after they closed up the shop, MacKenzie stopped by Ink to say goodbye to her friends and assure them that she would come by to visit. They were all there having a meeting and insisted she come in for a shot to say goodbye properly.

Zena, or Z for short, the owner of the incredibly popular tattoo parlor, was a very tiny woman, but the spectacular five-inch heels she wore almost everyday made her slight stature imperceivable. Her shoe collection could probably rival all three of the Kardashian women's collections combined. She had a wicked mane of long, white-blond hair with hot pink underneath and intermingled with the blond. And that face! Well, Z had a face that MacKenzie would describe as angelic. Perfect creamy, pale skin and the most beautiful blue eyes MacKenzie had ever seen.

MacKenzie had liked Z immediately. She was gregarious and kind. Jake and Owen looked like what you would consider traditional tattooed biker dudes, but really, they were sweethearts. Then of course there was Trina who, even after three shots and as she was walking out the door to go home, was telling her she was picking her up to go the club later that night. Laughingly, MacKenzie agreed because she was certain Trina had no idea where she lived.

Monday morning found her at the diner for a big breakfast and lots of black coffee. She didn't know what to expect for her first day except that it would be busy and hectic, so Ed's French toast and home fries would have to fuel her for most of the day, if not the whole day. In between orders, she told Ed she had landed the job and today was her first day. She admitted that she was nervous.

Ed smiled. "You'll do great, sweet pea," he said.

As she stood up to pay, Ed waved her away. "Naw, breakfast is on me, sweet pea. You just knock 'em dead," he said, sauntering back to the grill.

MacKenzie laughed. "Thanks, Ed, although I'm not sure that's the best phrase for a chef's first day of work. But I certainly understand your meaning, and I appreciate it," she said, chuckling as she walked out the door, mumbling under her breath, "Please, please, God, don't let me kill anybody with my baking today."

MacKenzie entered the restaurant dressed in her usual black slacks and pressed white button-down blouse with comfortable black heels. She knocked on Davey's office door, which was slightly ajar.

"Come in," Davey said absently.

MacKenzie walked in quietly. "Good morning," she said as softly as she could with her raspy voice.

Davey's head jerked up. "Oh hey! Good morning, have a seat please," he said, motioning toward the chairs in front of his desk. MacKenzie sat down and rested the apron she was carrying on her lap. Davey opened a folder and handed MacKenzie a stack of papers. "If you would look over the new-hire paperwork to start, and if you have any questions, just let me know," he said, finally looking her in the eyes.

Mackenzie felt a jolt when their eyes met, and her mouth went dry. "Oh, OK, sure," she said, picking up the paperwork and starting to read. She could only comprehend about half what she read because her pulse was racing, and she was finding it hard to breathe, let alone concentrate.

What she did discover was that the salary was very generous, as were sick time and vacation days. MacKenzie signed her name to all the papers and handed them back to Davey. Their fingers touched for the briefest of seconds, but it was enough to send a zing through her. Holy hell.

Davey looked slightly rattled when he asked, "Good, any questions?" without meeting her eyes.

"Um, nope. I didn't see any reference to human sacrifices, so I'm good," she said, smiling mischievously.

Davey looked up quickly to see her smile and never missed a beat. "Ah, I'm glad you didn't read the fine print," he said, genuinely smiling for the first time. MacKenzie laughed.

Davey showed her around the large kitchen and her smaller kitchen in the back with which she was already familiar. He pointed out the big bulletin board that held the special menus for the next two weeks, which was great for planning her dessert menu. Davey clapped his hands together signifying the end of the tour. "I will leave you to it, and if you have any questions, just come to my office. I will be there for the morning. I have meetings in the city this afternoon, but Luis will be in shortly to begin prep for tonight," Davey said.

"Um, he's a little scary. I don't think he likes me. When I was here baking the other day, he never spoke a word to me," MacKenzie whispered, looking around to see if he was there. She didn't want to say so, but she thought he looked like that character Machete. Scary dude.

Davey laughed. "I know he is intimidating and gruff, but he is the best at what he does, besides me of course, and he doesn't speak much English," he said.

MacKenzie thought back to when she had first started to make the apple crisp. Luis had mumbled that she was just a baby in Spanish. As much as MacKenzie had traveled and changed schools growing up, she had had to be adept at multiple languages. She was very fluent in Spanish, French, and Italian, which covered most of the languages spoken in the different countries she had lived in.

MacKenzie smiled and nodded. "So noted and will give a wide berth," she said as she started unpacking her bag for the day, which held her iPad, notebooks, and cookbooks, along with a giant canister of M&M's for her counter. She wasn't sure she could or would want to get through the day without at least a couple of handfuls of M&M's. She particularly loved the blue ones. Nobody would ever be able to convince her that the blue M&M's weren't just a tad sweeter than the others. She always ate the blue ones last.

When MacKenzie set the giant glass canister of M&M's on the counter, Davey lifted one eyebrow. MacKenzie tried to look stern and pointed to him. "Do not judge me, Davey Johnson," she said and laughed as he threw up his hands in surrender and walked to his office.

"I would never judge you, MacKenzie Rose," he called back.

MacKenzie stomped her foot. Oh! He must have gotten her middle name from her social security paperwork. Rats!

Dinner tonight was smoked salmon, so MacKenzie decided on something simple and light. She made a to-die-for lemon meringue pie, so it was a no-brainer. MacKenzie sat down at the counter and turned on her iPad to sketch out her dessert plan for the week. Along with her basic assortment of cake, pies, chocolate mousse, and custards, she would offer one special dessert to complement the special meal of the day. She calculated what ingredients she would need for the week and then did a quick inventory of the basic ingredients that would need to be refilled. MacKenzie grabbed an assortment of canvas bags and headed for the Corner Market, which was really a huge market of organic and fresh foods as well as a fully stocked supermarket.

MacKenzie made the last of the lemon meringue pies and stored them in the walk-in cooler. Several shelves in the cooler were set aside for her use. She was just beginning the three-tier chocolate cake when Luis arrived. He simply nodded to her and began working. MacKenzie had made a point of taking out her earbuds when he arrived, just in case he wanted to talk to her. She always wore her music when she was working. She had gotten in the habit during her exams in France. There was so much pressure with the master chefs watching all their moves that the only way she could calm herself was with her music. Once she put her music on, all the kitchen noise and the people running to and fro were tuned out, and she could simply create. She only listened to her music when she was working during the day and not in the evening during the busy dinner rush.

Luis didn't say a word to her, so she plugged herself back in and found her zone. She had no idea that when a particularly fast upbeat song played in her ear, she would bounce and sway to the music and sometimes sing a verse or two. When she was putting the finishing touches on her masterpiece chocolate cake, she felt someone standing beside her. MacKenzie jumped when she looked up to see Luis eyeing her chocolate cake suspiciously.

MacKenzie pulled out her earbuds quickly as Luis motioned to the cake and then the board with smoked salmon listed. It took a moment for MacKenzie to realize that he was asking if they were serving chocolate cake with salmon. MacKenzie laughed and shook her head as he narrowed his eyes in anger. He thought she was laughing at him. MacKenzie stopped at once, held up her hands, and took a deep breath. In perfect Spanish she said, "No, no, I'm so sorry! Can we start again? Hello, my name is MacKenzie, but my friends call me Mac. Please come with me." She led him to the cooler for him to inspect her lemon meringue pies. Luis looked shocked at her Spanish and also at the impressive sight of the lemony goodness. Luis smiled, and it totally transformed his appearance. He told her that he needed a break and asked her to have tea with him.

Neither Luis nor MacKenzie saw Davey come out of his office after he heard her voice. Davey's temper instantly flared when he observed Luis glaring at MacKenzie and pointing to the menu board. He was just about to intervene and tell Luis to back off when MacKenzie very smoothly switched to Spanish, and before he knew it, Luis was pouring MacKenzie a cup of tea. Davey shook his head and smiled. MacKenzie O'Riley was full of surprises, he thought as he went back into his office.

Luis asked MacKenzie about her Spanish, knowing it was mostly native and not learned out of a book. MacKenzie told him about growing up a military brat and that they had been stationed at Torrejón Air Base in Madrid for a year. Luis looked sad for a moment before he told her that he was from a very poor part of Madrid and he missed his country very much. MacKenzie confided that because she had moved around so much as a child, she didn't have many friends, so she would bake. That's where she'd discovered her passion to become a pastry chef.

As they were finishing up their tea, Gabe and Mario, the assistant cooks, arrived and stopped short when they saw Luis and MacKenzie having tea together. Luis stood and introduced her to Gabe and Mario, who appeared to be her age and seemed very happy to meet her. Gabe nudged Mario. "She is much hotter than Monsieur Lastat," Gabe said in Spanish.

MacKenzie laughed and said, "Thank you, I think. You're not so bad yourself," in perfect Spanish. Gabe and Mario looked shocked. Luis laughed and thumped Gabe on the head and told them to get to work. With heads down, Gabe and Mario apologized and began work.

MacKenzie plugged her earbuds back in and also got back to work. She thought a lovely English bread pudding would be pleasing to John Q. Public.

8

As the restaurant was closing, Davey ventured to the kitchen to ask MacKenzie how her first day had gone. She was just finishing putting everything away when he leaned on the counter. "Well, how was your first day?" he asked.

MacKenzie turned from the sink and smiled. "Great! I have only half a pie left from all the lemon meringue that I made, and the three-tier chocolate cake was a big hit," she said beaming. Her smile was completely disarming and scattered his brain a little. "Good. So you will come back tomorrow?" he asked with his hands folded, as if in prayer.

MacKenzie took her apron off and hung it up. "*Si*, I will be back. I probably won't be in quite so early tomorrow seeing I have all my ingredients and have pretty much acclimated myself to my surroundings. I think I will sleep like a baby tonight," she said, situating her messenger bag across her chest.

Luis walked over with a bottle of clear liquid and three glasses. "*Chula*, we must toast to the success of your first day," he said, pouring just a smidgen in each glass.

Davey looked at Luis, astonished. "Luis, no, I'm not sure that MacKenzie will like your secret stash of moonshine," he said and looked uncertainly at MacKenzie.

MacKenzie knew what she must do and lifted her glass in toast. "*Salud,*" she said and clinked glasses with Davey and Luis before downing the clear liquid. The burning sensation was immediate, and she wanted to spit the foul liquid out, but she swallowed, blew out a flame from her mouth, and smiled as her face turned red.

Luis laughed and slapped Davey on the back. "Finally! You chose well, my friend!" Luis said and went back to cleaning up.

Davey looked at MacKenzie concerned. "Really, are you OK? That stuff is nasty," he whispered.

MacKenzie whispered back, "I think there's a hole in my stomach now."

Davey laughed out loud, put his arm around MacKenzie, and walked her out to the sidewalk to hail her a cab. It felt nice with his arm around her. Like it was meant to be there.

Davey walked to his office and sank down in his chair. What the hell? In one day MacKenzie had created fabulous desserts that the customers had raved about and had his most curmudgeonly employee referring to her by a Spanish endearment and toasting her with his exclusive stock of homemade moonshine, which he had never shared with anyone before, except Davey. Did she cast her spell on everyone she met? Apparently, she did. He remembered walking out and seeing Gabe and Mario watching her shapely backside bobbing and swaying to the music she was listening to as she baked. He had wanted to punch them, but instead, he stood behind her and glared at the men so they got the clear message to get back to work. Jesus. Davey scrubbed his hands over his face as he remembered MacKenzie's fine derriere and smiled. Sweet Jesus, he needed a cold shower before he headed home.

— ~

Caleb took a pull off the beer. "So how is Mac?" he asked, waggling his eyebrows and smirking.

Davey scowled. "Back the fuck down, Caleb. You're not getting within a hundred feet of her," he growled. What had he been thinking, coming over to his brother's apartment instead of going home? The beauty of having a large family was that you usually could find someone to hang out with when you needed to; hell, he didn't know what he needed, but he was beginning to regret his decision to come over.

Garrett, the fifth Johnson boy, was an editor and owner of a big New York magazine called *Metro Gent*. He had stopped over on his way home along with Jared, their summer brother.

The apartment was occupied by Bobby and Ty, identical twin Johnson brothers, along with Caleb whenever he was in town and occasionally Henry when he was in town. Bobby was a doctor and worked very long hours, so it was a treat when he was able to hang with them. Ty had been a gifted baseball player and had been called up from the Portland Sea Dogs to play with the Boston Red Sox, but the week before he was actually going take the field, he had been in a motorcycle accident that left him with a permanent limp and crushed his playing dreams. It had been a horrible year trying to get him through that, along with Jack running away. A complete shitshow.

And then there was Caleb, the youngest Johnson boy. Caleb had more charisma and good looks than anybody had a right to, and boy, did he use it to the nth degree. Caleb was also a shit stirrer and had gotten his bell rung on multiple occasions because of his smart mouth. He worked for his family's athletic shoe business with his father and Marcus and Henry. Caleb traveled all over and took care of sales. He was a natural salesman and had made quite a name for himself in the industry. Caleb had always tried to get MacKenzie to date him when they were teenagers, but luckily, she had been smart enough to keep him at arm's length. Davey was going to make sure it stayed that way.

"Seriously, though, how is that working out?" Jared asked quietly. Jared had spent the most time with MacKenzie and Jack that summer before everything fell apart.

Davey took a pull off his beer. "She is the most amazing pastry chef and has completely charmed my most intimidating cook, so I guess you could say she's doing great."

Jared shifted in his seat and leaned forward with his arms resting on his knees. "Has she had any contact with Jack?" he asked uncomfortably.

Davey shook his head. "No, she was relieved when Jack was discovered and was doing well. MacKenzie just feels that if she hasn't contacted us boys then it is more than likely that she doesn't want to have contact with anyone from her past. She is hoping, like the rest of us, to reunite with her someday," Davey said.

Bobby walked over to the kitchen and pulled out a deck of cards from the drawer and held them up. "Texas Hold'em, No holds barred, boys. Lay your money on the table and smoke 'em if you got 'em," Bobby said smiling. Davey groaned. He knew he should have just gone home.

9

MacKenzie laid her organic fruits and other baking ingredients on the counter and smiled at the familiar grocery clerk, Jenny. On Mondays at the Corner Market, the staff was peppered with high-functioning individuals with Down syndrome. Jenny had singled MacKenzie out immediately as she was fascinated with Mackenzie's fiery red hair. But the fascination went both ways as MacKenzie was totally addicted to the excited yelp and running hug that Jenny gave her every Monday morning. There really wasn't a better way to start your week in her opinion.

She had been at Harmony for a month and loved the beautiful routine she had fallen into. She loved the job and the freedom that she had with her menu and the waitstaff, along with the kitchen staff. They were fast becoming her work family. She hadn't seen much of Davey because he had been traveling, but she also thought that maybe he was avoiding her somewhat. Whenever they were around each other, there was this electric vibration that couldn't be ignored. Davey would make some excuse up and retreat back to his office.

Two days a week, he cooked on Luis's days off, and MacKenzie had tried to not listen to her music, but it became so uncomfortable that she completely ruined a soufflé she was making. She had then just plugged her earbuds in and retreated within herself.

When Jenny was done ringing her up, MacKenzie asked her to walk with her out to the sidewalk. Jenny smiled and came around the counter. Arm in arm, they walked to the sidewalk. "How was your weekend?" MacKenzie asked.

Jenny smiled brightly. "I went for a long bike ride with my mom. I wanted to go to the Bronx Zoo, but my mom didn't have time," Jenny said.

They reached the sidewalk, and MacKenzie turned to Jenny. "Oh, I've wanted to go the Bronx Zoo since I got to New York, but I haven't had a chance. Maybe if it's OK with your mom, we could go together on Saturday."

Jenny screamed and hugged MacKenzie. MacKenzie laughed. "Have your mom call me this week, OK?" Jenny nodded and ran back into the market. MacKenzie smiled and turned around to find a sweaty Davey standing there watching her. She continued smiling. "Hi. Are you finishing your run or just starting out?" she asked, watching the sweat drip down his chin and drop to his soaked shirt. Sweet Jesus, his body was a thing to behold.

Davey cleared his throat, and MacKenzie's eyes darted back to his. "Do you know her?" he said, motioning toward the market.

MacKenzie looked confused. "Who? Oh, you mean Jenny? Yes, I have gotten to know her since I have been coming here on Mondays. She is fascinated with my red hair," MacKenzie said, touching the top of her head.

Davey looked intently at her. "I can see why, but I think it's more than that," he said softly. "Um, can I walk to the restaurant with you?" he continued, taking her canvas shopping bag.

"Yes, of course. I'd like that," she said shyly, and they walked toward the restaurant.

"I couldn't help overhearing you talking. Did you say you were going to the Bronx Zoo on Saturday?" Davey asked.

MacKenzie brightened and nodded. "Yes, if Jenny's mom says it's OK. I love zoos. My dad would always take me whenever we moved to a new location. It was kind of his way of apologizing to me for yet another relocation." MacKenzie shrugged. "I have been meaning to get to the Bronx Zoo since I moved here, but I just haven't taken the time."

Davey stopped outside the restaurant and turned to MacKenzie. "As long as I have lived here, I haven't taken the time either. Would it be too intrusive of me to ask to join you two on Saturday?" he asked.

MacKenzie was speechless for a minute before she shook her head and smiled. "No, not at all. I don't think there are any rules where zoos are concerned. The more, the merrier!" she said. They walked into the restaurant. This was going to be a fantastic week, MacKenzie thought as she put her ingredients away and started setting up for an amazing tiramisu for tonight.

10

ednesday was brutally busy, so MacKenzie helped out the waitstaff, getting drinks and keeping the coffee fresh. Davey had a meeting in the city and probably wouldn't be back to work tonight. Mike came out back after the restaurant closed and announced that there were dinner and drinks for anyone wanting to stay per Davey. Mike said he felt bad that he hadn't been there to help out and knew it had been crazy busy.

MacKenzie finished cleaning up and headed to the dining room to find many of the waitstaff and all the kitchen staff relaxing and having a drink.

Upon her arrival Mario jumped up and announced a new drinking game with shots and pongs. Before long there was a line on each side of the bar, and one line challenged the other in trying to bounce the ball into the shot glass. If the ball went in, the person who bounced it took a shot and the next player proceeded, down the line until one of the lines finished. The line that didn't win took another shot.

Well, after many shots later, Mike put on some music and the crowd started dancing. Mike pulled her from her seat, and they danced to Taylor Swift's "Shake It Off." MacKenzie was laughing and almost fell as Mike twirled her, and he caught her just before she lost her footing. As he was embracing her and letting her get her balance again, they looked up to see Davey standing there with his duffel bag, looking anything but happy.

MacKenzie smiled too brightly and waved to Davey. "Hi, are you going to join us?" she asked hopefully.

Davey looked at her flushed cheeks and then at Mike. "Um, Mike can I see you in my office, please? There are a few things I want to go over," he said, turning and walking toward the kitchen. MacKenzie stood there for a minute and then went to retrieve her hoodie and purse. It was time for her to go home. The walk to her house would be good to clear her head.

Luis put a hand on her shoulder. "Are you leaving, *chula*?" he asked. MacKenzie nodded. "*Si*, it's been a long day. I'll see you all tomorrow," she said, putting her earbuds in and pulling her hood up.

Davey walked back to his office and to the bathroom to change his clothes. Mike came in behind him and sat in the office chair. Davey left the bathroom door open so Mike could hear him.

"What's up, chief?" Mike asked.

Davey took a deep breath to try to calm himself. When he had come through the door and found Mike and MacKenzie in each other's arms, well, he had wanted to plant his fist in Mike's handsome face. "Pretty rowdy out there, isn't it?" Davey asked as he came out of the bathroom with his gym shorts and sweatshirt on. He sat down to put on his sneakers.

Mike shrugged. "It was a bitch of a day is all. Just blowing off steam, chief," he said with upturned hands.

Davey shifted uncomfortably, knowing Mike was right. It was nothing new to have drinks and a few laughs after a particularly trying day, but this was something more, and he would have to tread lightly so as to not raise any red flags. "Um, I saw you and MacKenzie out there, and I want to remind you about our unofficial policy on dating coworkers," Davey said, standing to lean on the back of the chair.

Mike looked confused. "We were just dancing, and she lost her balance. That's it, chief. Although I gotta say that if I was going to break that rule, I would totally consider breaking it with MacKenzie. She is

11

Davey had suggested that MacKenzie and he meet for breakfast, and of course MacKenzie told him there was only one place to breakfast at, and that was the Downtown Diner near her apartment.

The knock sounded at precisely nine o'clock. He was certainly punctual, MacKenzie thought. She had just finished getting ready and looked one last time in the full-length mirror in her loft. It was supposed to be hot today, so she had chosen khaki chino shorts with a simple white T-shirt and flip flops. She had thoroughly covered herself in sunscreen and brought some to reapply later. She popped her sunglasses on top of her head and climbed down the ladder. She was breathless when she answered the door. "Hi," she said, laughing in a breathless raspy voice. "That loft always challenges me. Are we all set?" she asked.

Davey swallowed. Jesus, he didn't want her to leave this apartment. She was friggin' gorgeous with her long creamy pale legs and the gentle curve of her hips up to the most perfect breasts he had ever seen. Not too big and certainly not too small—exactly perfect. When his eyes finally managed to reach hers, she was pink from blushing. So friggin' cute. "Um, yeah, all set," he said and waited for her to precede him down the hallway, which made him inwardly groan at having to watch her perfect derriere walk gracefully down the stairs.

MacKenzie was so turned on by watching him look her up and down that she was thankful he hadn't seen her doing the same. She drank in his black chino shorts that showcased his muscular legs and the black T-shirt that was snug across his broad chest. A tattoo showed beneath his shirt. He wore old well-worn boat shoes without socks. Yum. She could feel her face turn pink, and heat pooled in her sex. Deep breath. Deep breath.

MacKenzie expected to take a cab to pick up Jenny, but Davey walked toward a black Mercedes-Benz parked at the curb. He opened her door.

"This is yours?" she asked, clearly impressed.

He shook his head. "Nope. We're stealing it, but we will get it back before anyone notices," he said smirking. He got in and leaned over very close to her. MacKenzie caught her breath as their noses almost touched, and she could feel his breath on her face. Davey pulled the seatbelt across her lap. "Buckle up for safety," he whispered.

"Oh, thank you," she said and looked away as he started the car and weaved through traffic.

Jenny's mom was thrilled that MacKenzie was taking Jenny to the zoo. She was an older woman and tired easily. Jenny was in her thirties and high functioning, but she was still very active and excitable. As soon as MacKenzie and Davey were inside the brownstone, Jenny asked Davey if he had a cell phone. Davey indicated that he did indeed have a cell phone and Jenny's mom laughed and told Davey that under no circumstances was he to let Jenny have his cell phone because she would mess it all up pressing all the buttons. Jenny was fascinated by cell phones and asked everyone she met if she could borrow theirs. Sometimes she got lucky. Davey smiled and told Jenny maybe later. Jenny was perfectly happy with that answer and led the way to the car.

On the way to the zoo, Jenny peppered Davey with questions about his car but always came back to his cell phone and how much she would like to see it. MacKenzie laughed.

It was the perfect day for the zoo—a hot June day with a light breeze. The animals were a little lazy because of the heat, but they were still fun to look at. Jenny and MacKenzie both especially loved the monkeys, which were situated behind glass so you could get a really up-close view of their antics. Jenny would laugh when they jumped from branch to branch and squealed and that made MacKenzie laugh and finally Davey couldn't help but laugh at the monkeys as well. Davey bought them hamburgers and fries for lunch. Jenny and MacKenzie threw most of their fries to the seagulls that swooped down to get them. Each time Jenny would yell and cover her head.

When they had walked the park a full second time, Davey bought them ice cream, and they sat outside a little cafe and watched a zookeeper hosing down an elephant. Jenny yawned. MacKenzie looked at her watch and was shocked that it was so late in the day. "We better be getting you home, or your mom is going to worry," MacKenzie said to Jenny. Jenny hugged MacKenzie, leaving chocolate ice cream all over her white T-shirt. Davey watched MacKenzie look down at her shirt and laugh. MacKenzie looked at Jenny's face and still saw chocolate ice cream on her chin. She used the bottom of her white shirt to wipe the rest of the ice cream off Jenny's face.

Stunned, Davey was certain that no other woman he had dated would have ever done such a thing, and in fact, would have screamed that her shirt was stained beyond repair. His attraction to MacKenzie seemed to get stronger every day. He needed to make a decision as to whether he was going to let himself pursue it or not. He was a little afraid that that decision had already been made without his input.

Davey and MacKenzie dropped off a tired Jenny and then sat in the car trying to decide what to do for dinner. "Well, I am certainly not dressed to go out to dinner and honestly, I would really like something simple and light. I have a suggestion but you probably will think it's a terrible idea," she announced guardedly.

Davey smiled, enjoying the carefree manner of their conversation. There was something so comfortable about it. "Tell me. If you're offering to make me dinner, then it would have to be really horrible for me not to like your idea," he said, laughing.

"Well, I don't want to brag or anything, but I make a really amazing peanut butter and jelly sandwich served with a cold glass of milk. It's kind of my specialty," she said, shrugging.

Davey laughed out loud. He turned and leaned in close to MacKenzie. "Do you know how long it's been since I have had a PBJ with cold milk? God, I can't even remember. That sounds perfect to me. And, just thinking out loud here, but I'm sure there are many amazing things you can do," he said, in a whisper, looking into her eyes. MacKenzie held his gaze before looking away, blushing, and trying to hide a smile. Davey started the engine and drove toward MacKenzie's block.

— —

"Mm, so good," Davey moaned as he closed his eyes.

MacKenzie laughed. "I know, right? This, along with the entire day, will make my list tonight," she said, finishing her milk and walking to the sink to wash her glass.

"What list is that?" Davey asked. He was sitting at the bar.

MacKenzie turned around and leaned against the sink. "Well, when I was a child and right up until I went to France, almost every night, we had a family meal. My father may be the General, but my mother is commander in chief of our house, and she has always been adamant that we sit down to a family meal each evening. Sometimes it wasn't possible, but for the most part we did. During dinner each of us would have to tell five things they loved about their day. It could be as simple as watching a balloon released by a child float up into the clouds to winning the school spelling bee, which I did by the way. She just wanted all of us to notice the world around us. To step back from ourselves and observe and learn. When I went away to school, my mother asked me to continue our ritual each evening before I went to sleep, and she would do the same. She said it would link us together no matter where we were in the world. I still do it, and this day is at the top of my list."

Davey just sat there and stared.

"Thank you for sharing the day with me," she said softly.

After a minute of staring at each other, MacKenzie took a deep breath, picked up his glass, and turned around to wash it out. I shared too much, she thought. He must think I'm a sniveling baby. She needed to remember that not everybody had a dorky family life like she did.

Davey just stared at her back as he listened to his heartbeat thunder in his chest. He felt like he couldn't catch his breath. His gaze traveled down to the most perfect ass he had ever seen. Jesus, he needed to get out of there fast. He got up off the stool. "Well, I had better get going. I'm going to swing by the restaurant. I didn't hear from Mike today, so I'm assuming there were no fires to put out," he said, walking toward the door.

MacKenzie looked surprised. She wiped her hands dry and walked him to the door, peeked out the peephole into the hall, and then unlocked the door. When she turned around, Davey was smiling at her. "Am I safe to leave?" he asked.

"What? I always do that before I leave. It's important to know if there is any danger lurking in the hallway before you step out into it. You will thank me when you don't get mugged as you leave my apartment. But between you and me, I really do it to see if Mrs. Taylor from apartment thirty-four is out in the hall. She is lonely and loves to talk, and sometimes I just don't have the time, so I wait until she goes back into her apartment before I leave. So you can thank me for saving you from Mrs. Taylor, too. You're welcome," she said smirking and crossing her arms across her chest.

Davey had been laughing until she crossed her arms, which lifted her breasts together like an offering. His gaze traveled to her breasts and then back to her eyes, which now flared with heat.

Davey stepped close to Mackenzie, and she leaned back against the door. He put his arms on either side of the door above her head and leaned on the door, bringing his face practically nose to nose with hers. MacKenzie caught her breath and held his gaze. "What is this between us, MacKenzie Rose?" he whispered.

"I don't know," she whispered back.

"I want you. I want you more than I have ever wanted another woman, and I don't know what the hell to do about it." His breath warmed her lips. She parted them in welcome. Davey looked down at her lips and slowly back into her eyes.

MacKenzie's heartbeat was so loud that she was sure he could hear it. "I don't have relationships or girlfriends, MacKenzie. I date women once or twice, and I take them home and fuck them. Period. They know that up front. I don't mislead anyone. They want it as much as I do. There have been a few who thought they could get me to change my mind, but they can't, and I won't. I watched my father suffer for twenty years because he loved and lost. That will never happen to me. I won't let it. I love my life and don't want any more than what I have. Does it shock you to hear that I want to fuck you? That I want to rip those shorts right off you and fuck you hard, right against this door for Mrs. Taylor to hear?" he asked with a husky voice.

MacKenzie swallowed hard and shook her head. "I want you, too," she whispered, her eyes never leaving his.

Davey shook his head. "You deserve better than that and besides, it would break one of my big rules about not having sex with anyone I work with. I've learned my lesson the hard way, but I have never wanted anyone like I want you, so I want you to tell me to leave right now, MacKenzie, before I do something we both will regret." He looked down at her parted lips.

"I can't," she whispered.

Davey groaned, rested his forehead against hers, and closed his eyes. "Good night, MacKenzie Rose, and thank you for a lovely day and the amazing peanut butter and jelly sandwich. I'll see you at the market on Monday at ten o'clock," he whispered.

"Don't forget the milk," she said as she felt him move her away from the door.

"What?" he asked, looking confused with his hands still on her arms.

"You also had milk with your amazing PBJ," she said distractedly.

Davey smiled. "Good night," he said and walked out the door to find Mrs. Taylor just leaving her apartment.

"Well, hello, there, young man. Have you been visiting our MacKenzie? Lovely girl, she is," MacKenzie heard as she locked the door and smiled.

12

What. The. Hell. MacKenzie tossed and turned all night, trying to make sense of Davey's pronouncement. *I just fuck them. I watched my father suffer for twenty years alone.* Did he really believe that it was better to go through life never having loved someone? MacKenzie had always believed that there was a special man out there somewhere who would love her for all her quirkiness and sweep her off her feet just like in the books she read. She had to believe in happy endings, or what was there? A bland vanilla life. No way, no how. She wanted chocolate with rainbow jimmies, thank you very much!

MacKenzie sighed as she remembered the heat and passion that had roared through her body. She had never felt anything so powerful, not even with Roberto. Roberto had been an excellent lover. A true Italian, to be sure. He had always taken his time and made slow sweet love to her. It was nothing like what she felt with Davey. She wanted his hands on her like she wanted her next breath. Did he think less of her because she told him she wasn't shocked that he wanted to fuck her against the door? She would never look at her door in quite the same way again as she imagined being taken hard and fast by Davey. MacKenzie blew out a breath. It was clear that she wasn't getting to sleep anytime soon, so she kicked off the covers and padded to the ladder. She would make her dessert menu for next week; that should put her to sleep.

Sunday was lazy as she lay on a blanket under a tree in Central Park reading the novel *Poldark*. MacKenzie set the book beside her and sighed. If only love could be as simple as it was in 1800s, she thought wryly. Her cell phone rang a soft soothing sound of Beethoven. "Hello?" she answered.

"Hi, Mac, this is Trina. Where the hell have you been? We need to see you, and there will be a rowdy game of dirty drinking Scrabble as soon as you arrive. Like about thirty minutes," she demanded.

MacKenzie laughed and groaned. "Trina, I have to work tomorrow. I can't be hungover. Do you know how hard it is to work around food when you're hungover?"

"Oh, pish posh, never mind that. Just get your sexy little ass over here to SoHo, bitch!" Trina laughed.

"Fine, fine I'm heading to the subway now. Don't get your panties in a twist," MacKenzie chided.

"I can't because I don't wear any!" Trina said. MacKenzie laughed and hung up. She shook her head and smiled. Maybe this was exactly what she needed to take her mind off the confusing thoughts racing through her head.

13

avey checked his watch for the third time. Fifteen minutes late. He leaned against the Corner Market brick wall, waiting for MacKenzie to arrive. He was starting to worry. He had her phone number, but he didn't want her to think he was checking up on her work day. After all, this was her schedule and nothing she needed to stick to for the restaurant. She was able to keep her own schedule, and this was her Monday morning ritual. She was always very precise with her routines. He assumed because of her background of moving around so much and never knowing what the next day would hold, she stuck to her routines rigidly. This was definitely out of the norm for her, and he didn't like it. Finally, he caught sight of her walking briskly with her head down wearing sunglasses and carrying the canvas bags. Something was off.

She spotted him and stopped short. Ugh, why did he have to look so damn gorgeous? she thought, grimacing at the pounding in her head. She was never drinking or speaking to the crew at Ink ever again, she thought. "Hi. I hope you haven't waited long. I overslept a little," she explained in a low raspy voice.

As they walked into the market, he motioned to her sunglasses. "Why the sunglasses? It's not sunny, and we're in the store. Are you in disguise?" he whispered, leaning in, smiling.

MacKenzie scowled, lifted her sunglasses on top of her head, mumbled, "The bright light is hurting my eyes," and walked ahead. Davey caught up, stopped, and turned her to face him. Her eyes were bloodshot and tired, and she looked altogether peaked. "Are you ill? Why didn't you just stay in bed? You can't be around food or people if you're sick, MacKenzie," he said angrily.

"I don't have an illness," she said, grumpily walking ahead and picking up some pure vanilla extract off the shelf.

Davey caught up with her again and turned her to face him again. "What the hell does that mean? You look like hell, and you're pissy. Wait, someone didn't die or anything, did they? Did something happen?" he asked, changing from angry to concerned within seconds.

MacKenzie's temper flared instantly. "Jesus Christ, I'm not ill, I'm hungover! OK? Satisfied? I will be fine. Now can we please, please just shop in silence? Actually, why don't you just go, and I will meet you at the restaurant," she said, trying to sound calm.

Davey stood still with a shocked look on his face and his mouth hanging open. MacKenzie rolled her eyes and blew out a breath before starting up the aisle with her list. Seconds later, Davey was right beside her, taking the canvas bags from her with a huge smile on his face.

MacKenzie narrowed her eyes at him. "What?" she barked.

Davey just kept smiling. "Nothing," he said, holding open the bag for her to fill.

"Whatever," she muttered and finished shopping.

When they got to the checkout, MacKenzie asked the cashier where Jenny was today. "Oh, I think she is sick today," the cashier said. MacKenzie looked concerned.

When they got to the street, Davey had the bags, and he motioned for her to sit on the bench. "Call Jenny's mom, and see if Jenny is OK. I know you want to," he said softly.

MacKenzie looked into his eyes and nodded. The phone only rang twice before Jenny's mom picked up. "Hi, Mrs. Smith, it's me, MacKenzie. I am just leaving the Corner Market, and the cashier said Jenny was sick. Is she OK?" MacKenzie asked.

"Oh yes, MacKenzie, she will be fine. She just has a little cold start-ing, and I thought it best that she stay home and rest. Jenny is not happy about it. She loves working at the market and seeing you," she said.

MacKenzie smiled, relieved. "Oh, I'm glad that's all it is. I missed her as well and wanted to check on her. Would you tell her I said hello?" MacKenzie said, and Davey pointed to himself. "And tell her Davey says hello as well," she laughed.

"OK, fine, dear, I'll do that. Have a lovely day," Mrs. Smith said and hung up. MacKenzie took a deep breath and stood up. They walked to the restaurant in silence.

As MacKenzie and Davey entered the restaurant, Mike greeted them, looking surprised. "Hey chief, you're here early."

Davey looked uncomfortable. "Ah, yeah, we just had to get some stuff at the Corner Market," he said, walking briskly to the kitchen where Mario and Gabe were already working.

Mike followed Davey and MacKenzie into the kitchen. "Wait, you needed to pick up stuff? Is there someone who is not doing their job?" Mike asked.

Davey turned and looked directly at Mike with big eyes. "No, we're good," he said slowly.

A light went off with Mike, and he nodded and smiled. "Oh! OK, OK. I got you, chief," Mike said, smiling.

Davey turned around. "I have an announcement to make to all the kitchen staff, though," he said, talking too loudly for just the five of them in the kitchen. "MacKenzie has come to work with a hangover, so we must treat her as we treat all those who come in after drinking on a school night. And the first order of business is to put some music on, and I think we will make use of MacKenzie's iPod today."

MacKenzie was just about to plug in her earbuds. Davey stretched out his hand. Her head shot up. "Oh no! You can't make me give it to you, Davey!" she said, shaking her head.

"Oh, I'm pretty sure I can, sugar. Now hand it over peacefully, Miss O'Riley," Davey said, shaking his open hand.

MacKenzie glared at Davey. Davey smiled. Jesus, even green around the gills and spitting fire she was friggin' adorable. MacKenzie laid her iPod in his hand. "Here ya go, *sugar*," she said.

"Oh, and I almost forgot. I will be cooking on Mondays and Fridays. Luis wanted those days off for the summer," Davey said, picking up his apron and plugging MacKenzie's iPod into the dock. "Let's get this party started." He turned the volume up full blast.

MacKenzie groaned as Hanson blared "MMMBop," and Davey started dancing as he got out his ingredients. She would surely die of embarrassment or a migraine, she wasn't sure which. She stomped to her counter and began setting up for the day.

14

MacKenzie was eating her fluffernutter sandwich and milk in the break room by herself when Davey came in, turned a chair backward, and sat down beside her, setting her iPod down in front of her. "I think we have all been punished enough. They say you can tell a lot about a person by listening to their playlists," he said smirking.

MacKenzie tried to look bored and tried to speak, but the peanut butter got stuck in her throat, and she coughed. Davey patted her on the back. Great. Classy. MacKenzie took a big gulp of milk and cleared her throat. "If you had asked, I could have simply told you I was a dork," she said in a bored tone.

Davey laughed and took a napkin from the table. He leaned in close and wiped the full milk mustache off her lip. "You're not a dork. You're adorable," he said softly.

MacKenzie rolled her eyes. "Yeah, that's how all young women want to be perceived. Adorable," she said, taking another bite of her sandwich.

Just like that, Davey switched from playful to intense. He leaned in close to her ear. "Do not doubt for a second, MacKenzie, that along with adorable, I find you incredibly sexy. I can't stop thinking about every way in which I want to pleasure you with my mouth, my hands, and my hard-as-fuck dick. Are we quite clear about that?"

MacKenzie nodded slowly and tried to swallow. The peanut butter stuck again in her throat, and she coughed. Davey picked up her milk and handed it to her as she looked into his lustful eyes. She licked her lips. Davey let his chair fall back onto all four legs.

"Jesus, you're killing me, sweetheart," he said, standing up to leave. "As soon as the rush is done, I want you to go home and go to bed. No later than eight o'clock. Do you understand?" He looked concerned.

MacKenzie saluted with her sandwich. "Yes, sir."

Davey smiled. "I like that," he said as he was walking out.

MacKenzie had just taken a big bite of fluffernutter, so her "Don't get used to it" came out all garbled, but Davey got the message and laughed.

"At ease, soldier," he said and walked into his office.

The week flew by with sparks of sexual tension whenever Davey and MacKenzie were in the same room. Thursday night, after everyone had cleaned up, a group stayed to have a drink before going home. MacKenzie sat at the bar while Davey stood behind it, prepared to serve drinks. "What will the lady have?" he asked in his most aristocratic voice.

"Oh, a glass of house red, please," she said in her best British accent.

"Coming right up, m'lady," Davey said, pouring the wine. "So, tell me, m'lady, where did you go on Sunday night to get inebriated?" He set the wine in front of her.

MacKenzie's face turned red. "Um, I was visiting friends, and we played a drinking game," she mumbled as she took a sip of wine.

"What? Did you say a drinking game? Which one? I know all of them. And what part of the city were you in?" he asked, giving her his full attention.

MacKenzie shook her head. "No, really, I'm sure you haven't played this game. I was in SoHo," she said, wishing he would change the subject.

"SoHo? That's quite a ways from your apartment. Whereabouts in SoHo?" he asked, not giving up.

MacKenzie fidgeted uncomfortably and took another sip of wine. "Um, it's the tattoo parlor, Ink. I met the crew when I worked at the cupcake shop," she said not meeting his eyes.

Davey leaned on the counter starting to look angry. Someone down the counter asked for some whiskey. Davey just slid it down the counter, not taking his eyes off MacKenzie. He leaned down so no one could hear their conversation. "You were drinking shots in a tattoo parlor in SoHo?" he asked in a low growl.

MacKenzie squared her shoulders and sat up straighter. "Yes, I was. They just look rough around the edges, but they're all very nice, and they're my friends," she said stubbornly.

Davey still looked angry. "MacKenzie, you're too trusting. Did you take the subway home?"

MacKenzie shook her head. "No, I shared a cab with two women friends. Speaking of being too trusting, what about you, Davey? Can I trust you?" she asked, looking him in the eye intently.

The anger left his eyes and was instantly replaced with heat. "No, MacKenzie Rose, you shouldn't trust me," he said quietly.

MacKenzie finished her wine and handed him her glass. "Good night," she whispered. She said her goodbyes to the others and left the restaurant. Davey's eyes never left her as he watched her walk out the door. He sighed. He needed to go for a long night run followed by a very cold shower.

15

"I can't believe I'm letting you talk me into this," MacKenzie said, looking around Z's amazing walk-in closet in her beautiful apartment over the tattoo parlor.

Trina sighed. "Z won't go unless you go, and you just plain don't go out, period. I mean to change that." Trina held a slinky cocktail dress up to MacKenzie.

MacKenzie shook her head and looked at Z, who was lounging on the sofa. A friggin' sofa in your closet! "Help me out here, Z," MacKenzie said pleadingly.

Z laughed. "I know, sweetie. It's probably crazy, but Trina's right. I need to expand my horizons, and you just plain need to get a life. There's more to life than work and books," she said firmly.

MacKenzie harrumphed. "So says the woman who works twenty-four seven," she said, shaking her head at another barely there dress.

"I know! That's exactly what I'm talking about! We need to go out and have some fun. We're just going to check this place out. If we don't like it, we can leave and go somewhere else. Everyone is talking about this place. It's the hottest place going. Now we need to dress you. How do you want to be perceived? Sweet and innocent or sexy and dangerous?" Z asked.

MacKenzie's eyes widened. Oh, to not be "adorable" for just one night would be so great. "I want to be badass," she said looking at Z and then at Trina.

Trina let out a whoop. "Now we're talking!" she said, rummaging through the clothes racks.

MacKenzie stood in front of the four-way mirrors and just stared. She wore black leather pants with ridges going around each thigh, a white T-shirt, a formfitting black leather jacket zipped up but still showing cleavage, and a pair of strappy black four-inch heels. Z had curled and teased her hair into a mane of fire and finished with perfect makeup and smoky eyes that looked back at her in the mirror. "Wow, guys! I'm not sure I dare go anywhere like this. I feel like I'm part of a gang or about to do something illicit," MacKenzie exclaimed as she did a karate kick toward the mirror.

"Speak English, girlfriend. You look amazing, and I gotta say that I'd do ya," Trina said, laughing.

They all laughed. "No, really, MacKenzie you look amazing. We'll have fun tonight. OK? Deal?" Z asked, putting her arm around MacKenzie and looking at her in the mirror.

MacKenzie nodded and sighed. "You're both right. I need to get out there and start participating in this thing called life," she said, squaring her shoulders. "But nobody had better try to spank me, or I'm going to give them a karate kick." MacKenzie demonstrated in the mirror again.

Trina laughed. "You go, tiger."

— —

Davey walked out of his office, determined to ask MacKenzie to go for a drink with him. He had wrestled all week with the pros and cons of asking her on a date. Even after telling himself over and over that it was a bad idea, that they worked so well together he shouldn't do anything to mess that up, that he couldn't offer her anything other than a short physical relationship. Well, he *wouldn't* offer any more than that.

Every night, he tossed and turned, thinking about her and how she would feel beneath him, and every day, he found himself thinking about something she had said or the quirky little dances she did as she baked. Well, and then there was the staring; whenever she was in the room, he couldn't pull his eyes away from her. She was mesmerizing, and when she smiled, well, the entire room lit up. Jesus, he was going out of his mind with lust, and he needed to do something about it.

The decision made, he walked into the kitchen to find his assistant cooks, Gabe and Mario, alone. He walked out to the dining room and scanned the bar area. No MacKenzie. His eyes lit on a beautiful blonde at the bar who was looking at him invitingly. A few months ago, she would have been in his bed before the night was done, but tonight, she couldn't even tempt him as he looked for his fiery-haired MacKenzie. Wait, what? His MacKenzie? He needed to get MacKenzie beneath him so he could get past this intense desire and move on. That was it, just get her out of his system.

He walked back into the kitchen. "MacKenzie left?" Davey asked Gabe and Mario. When Mario nodded his head, Davey couldn't help feeling disappointed. They had had such a good time in the kitchen today. Davey had cooked, and they all joked around. It was amazing how well he and MacKenzie worked together. "Do you happen to know if she was going straight home?" Davey asked Mario.

Mario looked uncomfortable. "Um, I overheard her talking to her friend. I think they are going to that club Heaven," Mario said quietly.

Davey just looked at Mario stupidly before he sobered, then he nodded and stalked toward the door. Fuck, no. That was not going to happen. What the fuck was she thinking, going to an S&M club?

He jumped in his Benz and pulled out into traffic. No fucking way, he thought as his blood started to boil.

— ~

Marcus stood at the window and watched Davey pace back and forth on the sidewalk in front of the club. What the fuck was Davey doing here? he wondered. He had first seen Davey on the monitors in the bar and on the dance floors. He appeared to be looking for someone because as soon as he determined that that someone wasn't in the club, he had gone outside to wait and pace. This was certainly not a place that he had expected to ever see Davey. None of his family knew anything about this side of his life, and that's exactly the way he wanted to keep it. He ran his father's company, but he had wanted to do something on his own.

He had first been introduced to S&M on a business trip to Hong Kong many years ago and was hooked from the very first encounter. He thought a similar club in Manhattan would do well. He had been so right. In the year it had been open, the line to get into the club every night stretched down the street with many not even making it through the doors at all.

He had never expected to see his playboy chef brother come to his club. Marcus watched as Davey continued to pace back and forth. He was pissed. Marcus could tell by the set of his shoulders and the look on his face. All his siblings were extremely close and had gotten closer the past three years as they looked for their little sister who had run away. Jack, he thought with sadness. At least they knew she was safe and well.

Marcus watched as a cab pulled up to the curb. A beautiful white-blond-and-pink-haired woman stepped out of the cab wearing a white cocktail dress and killer high heels, followed by a punk rocker woman with black spikey hair and jeans with thigh-high boots. As Marcus continued to watch, what followed next was a pair of strappy black heels with diamond studs across the toes, black leather pants, and a leather jacket. As the third woman stepped out of the car, Marcus could see a full head of red curls. Mac. Marcus smiled as he watched Davey standing on the curb completely dumbstruck and then marching over to Mac.

MacKenzie looked up to see Davey standing in front of her with a scowl on his face. "Davey! What are you doing here?" she asked with big eyes.

Davey glared at her. "One could ask you the same, MacKenzie," he growled.

MacKenzie glared right back. "What? You think I should sit home with my books, Davey? Well, I'm tired of that. I'm going to go out and have some fun," she said, straightening up, her gaze never leaving his.

The heat left his gaze. "No, I don't want you to sit home with your books. I came out of my office tonight intending to ask you to come out with me, but you had already left. Without saying good night, I might add," he said softly, still holding her gaze.

MacKenzie's eyes got bigger and her mouth formed an O. "You were?" she asked unbelievingly.

Davey smiled. "Yes, I was. And if you had said yes, I was going to bring you to a special place I think you will really love. Will you come with me, MacKenzie?" Davey asked, looking hopeful.

MacKenzie looked at Davey and then at her friends, who were watching the scene intently. Z laughed and came over and hugged MacKenzie. "Have a good time, and you owe me big time for bugging out on me and leaving me to this den of inequity," she whispered in her ear. MacKenzie smiled and nodded.

Z held out her hand. "I'm Zena, but everyone calls me Z. Take good care of our Mac," she said, shaking Davey's hand.

Davey nodded and smiled. "Of course. I promise she's in good hands. Nice to meet you."

Trina just walked up until she was practically nose to nose with Davey. "I'm Trina, and if you hurt her, I'll hurt you," she said and hugged MacKenzie.

Davey looked down and tried to hide his smile. "So noted," he replied and held out his hand to MacKenzie as he walked her to his car.

16

oly fuck. He never would have guessed the fuck-me heels and leather getting out of the cab belonged to his MacKenzie. There it was again, *his* MacKenzie. But when the fiery-red curls and come-hither eyes met his, he was speechless. She was the most gorgeous woman he had ever seen, and his instinct to grab her and get her away from all other eyes was intense. After a terse exchange, thank God she had accepted his offer to come with him, or he would have had to stay and beat every man who approached her. He had been fully prepared to do just that, but he much preferred to take her to a special blues club on the Upper East Side that he had discovered last year. Listening to her iPod playlist while they worked a few weeks back, he had noticed quite a few blues numbers in her mix. She was an enigma, his MacKenzie.

They rode in silence. As Davey was helping her out of the car, he held her hand, brought her in close, and whispered in her ear, "Thank you for coming with me tonight. I think you will really like this place."

MacKenzie smiled. "Well, let's go find out, shall we?"

Davey smiled and held her hand as he walked her through the heavy metal door and down the stairs. It was dark, and the music hit MacKenzie like a warm breeze. A soft and soulful melody came from a tall dark-skinned woman holding a standup mike like it was the face of a lover. MacKenzie was immediately captivated. She turned to Davey with a surprised look to find him watching her intently. "I love it already! Thank you." she whispered.

Davey smiled. "I thought you might," he said, and he led her to a table against the wall.

The waitress came over, and Davey ordered a house red for MacKenzie and a scotch neat for himself. They sat close together, and he hadn't yet released her hand. MacKenzie just let herself feel the music. It felt so right being here sharing this with Davey. She felt like he understood her as no one had before. She wasn't just a dorky army brat with books for friends. She felt like a sexy, desirable woman he wanted to spend the evening with. A warm feeling in the pit of her stomach that was present whenever she was around Davey or even thought of him blossomed until it threatened to overwhelm her.

She leaned over and rested her head on his shoulder. "This is lovely," she whispered.

Davey turned his head and caught the fragrance of her hair along with her perfume. It hit him, making him take a sharp intake of breath, and he grew harder, which he would have bet money wouldn't have been possible, seeing how he had been rock hard the moment he saw MacKenzie standing on the sidewalk after she got out of the cab.

"MacKenzie," he whispered into her hair. MacKenzie turned her head to look him in the eyes. Their gazes locked, and the heat sizzled in the air between them. He looked down at her parted lips and moaned. His hands came up to hold her face gently, and he lowered his lips. The moment their lips touched, Davey moaned, wanting to deepen the kiss but holding back, not wanting to scare her with his desire. The truth was that all he wanted to do was strip her naked, take in all her glorious body, and fuck her like a rutting bull.

Instead, Davey kissed her softly, tasting her lips and the sweet wine she was drinking. She wanted more, and as he teased her mouth, her tongue came out, tasted his lips, and skimmed inside his mouth. Davey moaned, not able to take any more, and deepened the kiss, driving his tongue inside her mouth to taste all of her. MacKenzie moaned deep in her throat, which made Davey break contact and press their fore-heads together, breathing deeply. When she had moaned, he could easily have come in his pants from just that throaty sound. Jesus Christ. He had been reduced to a sixteen-year-old. "What are you doing to me, MacKenzie Rose?" he asked, just as the singer finished the first set.

They broke apart to clap and take a sip of their drinks. Davey eyed her over his glass, and his eyes narrowed.

MacKenzie took a sip of wine. "What?" she asked in a raspy tone.

Davey set his drink down, still eyeing her. "Can I ask you some-thing? You don't have to answer if you don't want to," he said, leaning toward her.

She leaned toward him, smiling. "Sounds ominous," she said.

Davey looked serious. "What made you come to New York? Why would you give up an internship at the prestigious La Pergola in Venice to come to New York and make cupcakes in SoHo?" he asked.

MacKenzie sighed. "I was wondering when you were going to ask me that." Her smile didn't reach her eyes. She sighed again. "Why else? A man," she said, looking away.

Davey saw hurt in her eyes, and his guts churned with jealousy and anger on her behalf. MacKenzie looked back at Davey and was surprised at his angry expression.

"As you know, growing up I moved around a lot, and by a lot, I mean *a lot*. Sometimes we weren't in the same location more than six months before uprooting. And like you probably already know or pre-sume, I didn't have many friends. There was this Italian boy my age, and his father was high up in the government like mine, so we were thrown together quite a lot. We became fast friends at an early age. When we weren't together, we would skype or e-mail each other. It was very difficult for Roberto—that's his name—to have friends as well be-cause of his family. Until Jack came along, Roberto was really my only close friend.

"Well, when Jack was sent away, and I went to France to culinary school, Roberto persuaded his parents to let him go to college in France. We began to spend every day together, and he began to change toward me. At first, it was just little things, like him being jealous if a man looked at me or, god forbid, spoke to me, and he would hug me tighter and longer when we would say goodbye in the evening. But it wasn't until he kissed me that I got angry and asked him what he was doing. He told me that he loved me and that he had for some time. He wanted us to be a couple and perhaps marry one day. I told him that was crazy talk and to just stop. I told him I loved him like the best friend that he was, but nothing more. He promised that he could make me love him in time, and he begged me to give him time. I don't know if it was his proclamation of love of which I had only read in books, or his look of desperation that he would now lose me as a friend, but I gave in and told him that, although I didn't feel that kind of love for him then, I wouldn't close to the door to it for the future. Although at the time I was certain that my emotions would remain the same.

"Well, as the year went on, he did indeed sweep me off my feet. Roberto is a full-blooded Italian and doesn't do anything half measure. Eventually, we became lovers, and I fell in love with him. I received the internship at La Pergola, which I think he was responsible for, but I was so happy I didn't care enough to question it. I told my parents that I thought Roberto was close to proposing, and my mother was over the moon about it. Both my parents had known him since he was a child, and they got on well with his family.

"Well, one day I was at work and started feeling poorly, so I decided to go home. But instead of going home, I went to Roberto's apartment to rest because it was closer than mine. I had my own key, so I let myself in and went straight to the bedroom, where I walked in on Roberto in a very compromising position with a leggy brunette. I ran out of the apartment before he could even get dressed. I called my dad and told him what happened and that I needed to come home. I got passage on a military jet, and I was home within forty-eight hours. I've never seen the General so angry. After Roberto called the first time and the General answered, well, he never called back. I had been home only about two weeks when I realized I couldn't stay there. As much as I love Harmony, Maine, there isn't much work for a pastry chef.

"I was moaning about my situation to Charlotte one day; Charlotte and I roomed together at Gastronomicom in France. She offered for me to come to New York and take over the baking in her cupcake shop because she was pregnant, and her new rich husband didn't want her working so hard. So it was a win-win all around. Charlotte appeased her husband, and I got a job and a new start in New York." Mackenzie splayed her hands to gesture the end of the story. "Regret asking now?" she asked with a sad smile.

Davey took her hand and brought it to his lips. "He's a fucking idiot," he said, looking at her as he kissed her palm.

MacKenzie caught her breath as heat exploded in her belly. She smiled. "I believe that's the nicest thing anybody has ever said to me."

"It's true," Davey said, putting his arm around her and settling in as the next set began. The slow boil that Davey was feeling made him want to punch something or someone—namely Roberto, the fucking Italian jackass. It bothered him more than it should have to see the hurt in her eyes as she told her story. He was sorry he had brought up such an ugly memory for her. He felt this intense need to protect her, protect what was his. He might as well stop fighting this because she was under his skin, and no amount of willpower was going to keep him away from her. His desire was just too great. This was just going to have to play itself out.

When the last set finished, Davey led MacKenzie outside to the car. The cool air was refreshing after being down in a basement for several hours. Davey held onto MacKenzie's hand as he drove to her apartment. When he parked at the curb, MacKenzie asked him to come up for coffee.

He kissed her hand. "No, I'll pass tonight, but I will walk you to your door, Miss O'Riley. Now stay there while I get your door." He laid her hand in her lap, jumped out, and jogged around the car to open her door. He held out his hand. MacKenzie took it, and he all but lifted her out of the car and into his arms. "Did I tell you tonight how fucking sexy you look in that outfit? You almost brought me to my friggin' knees, MacKenzie," he growled in her ear.

MacKenzie giggled. "Why, thank you, Mr. Johnson. You tend to make my knees go a little weak yourself," she said shyly. Davey put his arm around her and walked her into the apartment building. When they reached her apartment, MacKenzie turned to face him. "Thank you, Davey. I had the most wonderful evening."

Davey just stared at her and then dropped his head to taste her lips. MacKenzie met his kiss urgently. She had been burning up since the kiss in the club. She rose up on tiptoe to get as close to him as she could. She wound her hands into his silky hair. Davey moaned, pushed her against her door, and ground his hardness against her core. They nipped at each other's lips, and their tongues danced and twisted against each other as they both moaned in need. Davey picked MacKenzie up, and she wrapped her legs around him. He pushed his hardness against her in a steady rhythm as he put his hand up her shirt and pulled her bra down so he could cup her full breast. Jesus. Her nipple was pebbled, and he flicked it and soothed it with the pad of his thumb.

MacKenzie moaned loudly and arched her back. "Davey," she whispered urgently. "I need more," she pleaded.

Davey kept up his rhythm at her core and kneaded her breast, wishing he could suck on it. "Shhh, I know, baby," he whispered as he took her mouth again, knowing she was going to come soon. As soon as his tongue entered her mouth, MacKenzie moaned long and loud. Her body stiffened, and her back bowed. She let her head fall back against the door. Her eyes were closed, her lips parted, and a pink flush spread from her neck to her hairline. She was fucking spectacular. MacKenzie opened her eyes, surprised, and let her legs fall to the floor. She wobbled a little unsteadily. Davey held her up.

"Are you OK? Steady now?" he asked, smiling.

MacKenzie smiled back. "Um, yeah, I'm good, but what about you? You didn't exactly…"

Davey put his finger over her lips. "I'm OK. Jesus, MacKenzie, I all but fucked you against your hallway door. I don't want our first time to be like that. I don't have any willpower where you're concerned. Come to Maine with me tomorrow morning. Marcus has his own plane; well, it belongs to all of us, really—the company, you know—but he is in New York tonight and flying back to Portland in the morning. He is coming back on Monday, so we can hitch a ride back with him. No one is at camp this weekend, so you could see your parents, and we could enjoy the weekend together," he said rubbing her lower lip. "Come on, what do you say?"

MacKenzie laughed. "This is madness," she whispered as she looked into his eyes. "But yes! It sounds like fun. Although I can't visit with my parents; they're out of town."

"Well, then, I will have you all to myself, won't I?" he said slyly. Davey turned serious. "MacKenzie, you know what I'm asking, right? You know that I want you more than I want to breathe right now?" He gently kissed her.

MacKenzie nodded. "I know what you're asking, and I want you, too," she said.

Davey had the biggest smile on his face. "Great! I will pick you up here at six a.m., and don't pack too many clothes. You're not going to need them." He took the key from MacKenzie's hand and unlocked her apartment door. "Now go sleep because I don't intend on letting you sleep much in the next twenty-four hours," he said. He gave her a quick kiss and walked toward the stairs. He pointed to Mrs. Smith's door and mouthed, "Do you suppose she heard you moaning?" He was smiling.

MacKenzie looked shocked. "You're a wicked, wicked man, Davey Johnson!" she whispered loudly and closed her door.

17

MacKenzie was sitting on the stoop when Davey pulled up to the curb. He jumped out to meet her with a big smile on his face. He was dressed in worn Levi jeans with a black T-shirt and worn leather boat shoes without any socks. His hair was still wet from his shower. Yum. MacKenzie smiled and handed him her duffel bag. He put his arm around her and kissed her. The moment their lips touched, a spark ignited, and the kiss deepened. Davey dropped her duffel and embraced her face with his hands. They both moaned.

Davey broke the kiss and just looked into MacKenzie's eyes. "Jesus," he said, out of breath. "Let's go quick." He pulled her to the car.

MacKenzie laughed. She had worn a simple summer dress that was comfortable and practical for traveling. When they arrived at the airport, they were led through a side door and straight onto the jet. It was small, but it would fit about twelve people. Marcus was already on the plane when she and Davey boarded.

He smiled and embraced MacKenzie. "Mac, it's really good to see you. You look amazing," he said.

Davey led MacKenzie to the double seats across from Marcus. "Back off, bro, she's taken," Davey said, hugging him.

Marcus laughed and held up his hands. "OK, but I'm not sure it will be so easy when Caleb sees MacKenzie," Marcus said laughing.

Davey scowled. "Fucking whore dog," he growled.

Marcus laughed harder. "So tell me, MacKenzie, what have you been doing with yourself for the past three years?"

MacKenzie told him about her culinary schooling and her internship and before she knew it, they were landing in Portland, Maine.

All three drove to the estate in Portland to drop Marcus off. Davey didn't even get out of the Suburban; he just waited for Marcus to grab his briefcase. "See you Monday, bro! Thanks for the ride!" Davey hollered as they drove away. Marcus smiled and waved.

They listened to a blues station on the way to Harmony. Davey stopped at the grocery store, and they picked up food for the next twenty-four hours. When they drove into camp, it was still barely morning. They raced into the camp and put away the food. "You go get your suit on, and I will pack us some beers and snacks and pick you up out front on the four-wheeler." He kissed her. "Or you don't have to wear a bathing suit at all. I'm really flexible like that," he said, smirking.

MacKenzie ran into the bathroom. "Not bloody likely," she hollered back to him.

When Davey took his shirt off on the beach, MacKenzie's mouth went dry. Bloody hell, he was gorgeous. He was lean and muscular with just a scattering of hair on his chest. The military recognition tattoo on his bicep was beautiful. MacKenzie wasn't the only one looking her fill. MacKenzie took off her shorts and T-shirt, revealing a black bikini, which instantly had Davey looking at her with intense heat in his eyes. They stood like that for a few moments, drinking each other in. "You know this is torture for me, don't you, MacKenzie?" Davey asked softly.

MacKenzie nodded. "I'm sorry, but the last one in the water is still the rotten egg," she said, taking off running toward the water.

"Shit!" Davey yelled and took off after her, quickly catching her as they both fell into the water. MacKenzie yelled and went under. Davey pulled her up from under the water and held her against him. MacKenzie wound her arms and legs around him and took his mouth in a demanding kiss. After her tongue found the inside of his mouth and tasted him thoroughly, MacKenzie broke the kiss.

"If you keep kissing me like that, I'm going to pick you up and take you to the beach and fuck you until you beg for mercy," Davey said in a husky voice. "You will have sand in places you don't want sand to be, my love. I have very little willpower when it comes to you, and what will-power I do possess is teetering precariously close to the edge."

MacKenzie smiled and shoved off him, swimming toward the float.

"Chicken," Davey said after her and swam toward the float as well.

They spent the entire afternoon swimming and lying on the float, just drifting in and out of sleep. Every once in a while, MacKenzie would feel Davey's lips on her stomach, or he would let his fingertips travel down the length of her body.

The sun was setting as Mackenzie leaned over and kissed Davey on his chest. She thought he was dozing, but he quickly rolled her over and was on top of her. She yelped and laughed. MacKenzie instantly felt his hard arousal and raised her hips to meet his. Davey moaned and dipped his head down. He moved her bikini off her breast, replacing it with his mouth. He sucked and moaned louder.

"Mmm, do you know how much I've wanted to do that? Please, MacKenzie, we need to get back to the house. I can't stand much more of this," he said in a pained voice.

"Yes, let's go now," she whispered.

They dove into the water and swam for shore. Davey drove the four-wheeler fast up the dirt road to the house. When they entered the house, Davey turned to her. "Will you come shower with me?" he asked. MacKenzie nodded and they walked to the bathroom.

As they stripped down, MacKenzie couldn't help but stare at Davey's incredible body and impressive hard manhood. Davey was watching her when her eyes caught his. "You're beautiful, Davey," she whispered.

Davey walked to her, untied her bikini top, and let it fall to the floor. He kneeled down and pulled her bottoms down, exposing the small patch of red hair covering her sex. Davey grasped her by the hips and kissed the hair on her pubic bone. "You are the beautiful one. I have never seen a more exquisite body in my life. How the images in my head have tortured me," he said, standing and pulling her into the shower.

The hot spray beat down on them as Davey got the soap and started lathering MacKenzie's body, taking his time and covering every square inch of her, making her squirm with need. MacKenzie took the soap from him and began slowly soaping him up all over. She kneeled and washed his manhood and legs, and as he rinsed, she looked up at him, took his cock in her hands, and licked the tip.

Davey shuddered and pulled her up. "That I couldn't handle right now. I would last about two minutes, if that," he growled as he shut the water off. Without toweling off, Davey picked MacKenzie up, walked to his bedroom, and closed the door. He laid her down gently on the bed and kissed her deeply. He slowly kissed down to her breasts, where he took his time and sucked and lapped each one until MacKenzie was crying out with need.

"Davey! I can't take anymore. I need you!" MacKenzie moaned.

Davey continued to kiss down her belly. "Shhh, I know, baby. I need to get you ready for me. Just enjoy," he said as he spread her legs and lapped at her core for the first time, bringing her up off the bed. MacKenzie caught her breath and moaned as he began to taste her in earnest. It seemed like only seconds before she was shattering into a million pieces. Davey crawled up her body and kissed her.

He reached toward the nightstand but MacKenzie stayed his hand. "I'm clean and have been on the pill for some time."

Davey stilled. "I'm clean, too. Are you sure, MacKenzie? I've never had sex without protection," he said, softly kissing her lips.

"I'm sure. I want to feel you inside me, Davey," MacKenzie whispered.

"God, I can't stand this any longer. I will try to be gentle with you, baby, but I've never been wound so tight before. Spread your legs wide for me, baby."

Davey took her mouth and plunged into her. They both moaned loudly. Davey didn't move. "Did I hurt you, sweetheart? You're so tight. Talk to me, MacKenzie," he said in an urgent voice.

MacKenzie moaned and moved her hips up to his. "Davey, I need you to move, please. I need more," she cried.

Davey moaned and began driving into her. "Oh, Jesus, MacKenzie, I've never felt anything like this. The feel of you without any barrier is too much. I'm not going to last, sweetheart!" he cried.

MacKenzie met him thrust for thrust. "Oh, Davey, don't stop! I can't stand it! Oh!" And she fell over the edge, moaning and gasping.

Feeling her sex clenching and tightening around him sent Davey right over the edge with her as he cried out her name. He rolled over and brought her with him in his embrace as they caught their breath, reeling at the intensity of the joining. He stroked her back. "You must be starved. I am," he said into her hair.

"Mmm, actually, I'm quite satiated at the moment," she sighed.

"Mmm, that was amazing. I'm so glad we're playing this out and not pretending there's nothing between us." He chuckled contentedly.

MacKenzie frowned and lifted her head. "Playing this out? What does that mean? It sounds like you expect what we feel to just fizzle out."

Davey shifted uncomfortably and put his arm behind his head as he continued to stroke MacKenzie's backside. "Well, it does eventually die. Which is probably a good thing because we would die of pleasure."

MacKenzie looked serious. "Davey, what if it doesn't fizzle out? What then?"

Let's not talk about this right now. Let's just enjoy each other."

MacKenzie sat up on her knees without any embarrassment. "I think it should be discussed. I think I need to know. What happens if it doesn't fizzle out?"

Davey looked at the ceiling, not able to look her in the eye. "I end it, MacKenzie. I thought we both knew what this was. I'm not a relationship guy. That's my choice, and I'm not going to change my mind. I watched my father suffer for more than twenty years after my mother died. I will never let myself fall that hard or suffer like he did. We're friends with an incredible sexual chemistry, so I thought that when the chemistry left, we would still be friends. Was I wrong?"

Friends. That hit MacKenzie square in the gut. "So this is just kind of an extended one-night stand? Did I have an expiration date, Davey?" She was fighting back tears. "I didn't think you'd be so shortsighted that if you met someone and fell in love, you wouldn't *want* to push that person away, but you're saying that no matter what, it ends."

"MacKenzie, I will never let it get to that point. I will never let myself fall in love. It's too destructive. Why would anyone put themselves through that hell? I won't do it. I don't want a relationship, marriage, or children. I won't change my mind."

The tears did start to fall, and Davey looked like he was in pain watching her. "Yeah, I'm sorry, too, Davey. I do want those things. All of them in excess, and I won't settle for anything less. Can I tell you something?"

He started toward her; she held up her hand.

"No, don't. I'm fine. When I walked in on Roberto at his apartment, it hurt like hell, but what hurt most was the loss of my best friend. You know I don't have many friends, so what friends I do have, I am fiercely loyal to and protective of. I was so angry at him for breaking that bond. He made me love him, and then he betrayed me. More than losing a lover, I mourned losing a friend. So no, Davey, I'm still your friend, and I thank you for setting me straight now instead of later. You'll have to give me a little time to adjust, though. You see, I am in love with you, which is why I wanted to make love with you. I respect your wishes, but I'm afraid I can't be a friend with benefits. I want more for myself than that. If you don't mind, I would like you to drive me to my parents' house for the night. I will see you at the airport." She walked out of the bedroom and out to wait by the truck.

Davey came out and leaned on the hood of the truck. "MacKenzie, please just come inside, and we'll make dinner. You need to eat something. Please."

MacKenzie shook her head. "No, Davey. Please just take me to my parents' house. I promise I will be fine," she said, climbing into the truck.

Davey drove his fist into the hood, making MacKenzie jump. "Jesus, you're stubborn!" he muttered. He climbed in the truck and sped to town much too fast. Neither spoke. At her parents' house, MacKenzie silently got out of the truck and turned the lights on, waiting for Davey to leave. He sat there for about ten minutes with the truck running before he squealed out of the driveway like a teenager. MacKenzie ran up the stairs into her old room, threw herself onto her bed, and cried as her heart broke into a thousand pieces.

Davey drove down to the lake and started a fire in the pit. Jesus, he felt like shit. He couldn't remember ever feeling like this, ever. What the fuck? He thought she knew how these things went. He hadn't wanted to hurt her. He felt sick at the thought of it. His phone was sitting on a stump. He kept looking at it. He wanted to call her. To make sure she was OK. He wanted to hear her voice. He sighed and kept remembering her moans as they'd made love. Had sex. They had sex. They fucked. No matter how great it was, it still was sex. Right?

Davey pulled out the bottle of Jack and poured a drink. If there was one thing he was certain of, it was that MacKenzie Rose O'Riley was not going to call him tonight. He thought of her tears and downed the whiskey, feeling it burn all the way down.

———

When MacKenzie had no tears left, she sat up, went into the bathroom, washed her face, and squared her shoulders. She could do this. She'd done it before, but this time, she wasn't running away. She was strong enough to put this behind her. She loved her job and her coworkers. She went downstairs and looked through the movies. She needed her best pick-me-up movie. Her hand automatically reached for *Pride and Prejudice* with Colin Firth. She desperately needed Mr. Darcy. She thought she should try to rummage through her parents' freezer to find something to eat, but she just wasn't hungry. She plugged in the miniseries, and before the five hours were up, she was fast asleep and never saw Elizabeth and Mr. Darcy marry. Pity, it was her favorite part.

18

MacKenzie heard a knock at the door. She stretched and opened her eyes to hear the knock again a little more aggressively. She jumped up from the couch that she had fallen asleep on. She sat up quickly, gathering herself she opened the door. "What time is it? Are we going to meet Marcus today?" she asked in her raspier-than-usual voice.

Davey sat back on his heels. "No, I just wanted to see you." He held up the jacket for *Pride and Prejudice*. "I missed a good time, I see," he said with a small smile, testing the waters.

MacKenzie smiled and nodded. "You sure did. Mr. Darcy will always be the man of my dreams. The bar is very high indeed."

A pang of jealousy hit him. Jesus, get a grip. It's a fictional character. And besides, he had no right to have any jealous feeling toward MacKenzie. He had given up that right last night. He needed to make their friendship right, though, right now.

"MacKenzie, I'm sorry if you think I misled you. I never, ever want to hurt you or make you cry. Jesus, that just about killed me. Please say our friendship is intact," he said nervously.

MacKenzie had never seen Davey rattled or nervous about anything. She took a deep breath. "Yes, our friendship is secure. I meant what I said, Davey. I don't take friendship lightly."

Davey stood up and held out his hand. "Good, because I feel the same, and friends spend time together, so I would like very much if you spent the day with me, starting with breakfast at the diner."

She looked at him. God, she loved him. It would hurt being around him today, but she also wanted—no, craved—his presence. When they got back to New York, she would begin to distance herself. Today, she would enjoy the day with him.

She nodded. "Let me shower, and I will be ready in thirty," she said, bolting upstairs.

Davey smiled and rocked back on his heels. She was even more beautiful when she woke up in the morning with her sleepy eyes and messed-up hair. He could feel her poking at his heart. He would give himself today with her, and then when they got back to New York, he would put some distance between them. The chemistry would simply die away if he ignored it. The image of her stretching as she woke up made him hard. Yeah, it will simply go away, he thought, mocking himself.

Davey and MacKenzie walked into the diner to find Gracie, the owner and dear friend of the Johnson's and O'Riley's, right out straight, but she ran over and gave them both a big hug. MacKenzie ordered pancakes with strawberries and whipped cream, and Davey ordered the bacon, home fries, and eggs platter. MacKenzie had forgotten how delicious the food was at the diner. She ate every bite, and as she shoveled the last of the pancakes into her mouth, she looked up to find Davey watching her.

"What?" she mumbled, her mouth full. She swallowed and took a sip of coffee. "I didn't realize how hungry I was."

He took her hand and held it. "I'm sorry about dinner last night. I wanted to cook for you."

MacKenzie pulled her hand back and picked up her coffee cup with both hands. "No worries. My belly is full now. What would you like to do today? It looks like another perfect summer day," she said, changing the subject.

Davey swallowed, feeling a hollowness in his gut. She didn't want him touching her. He finished his coffee. "I thought I would take you out in the boat today and putt around the pond," he said.

MacKenzie smiled, which lit up her entire face and made his insides twist. "That sounds perfect. Ready?" she asked, getting up. MacKenzie and Davey hugged Gracie as they left.

The sun hummed as they lay on the front of the boat, soaking up the heat. "Can I ask you a question, Davey?" Mackenzie asked.

Davey stirred sleepily. "Of course."

"Where is Bebe?" she asked quietly. Bebe had been Jack's mothers best friend and nanny to every Johnson child. To Jack and the youngest, she was the only mother figure they ever knew.

Davey cleared his throat and turned over on his side to face her.

"She is back in France. She was so angry at my father after he sent Jack away. After we found out that Jack ran away from Beckett's House, the halfway house Dad sent her to, Bebe felt there was no need for her here anymore, and she went back to the convent she lived in when she met my mother. I haven't heard anything recently," he said, lying back down.

Davey and MacKenzie swam and then looked for painted turtles sunning themselves on logs. When the sun was setting, they docked the boat and went back to the camp to cook dinner. Davey made pasta salad and grilled red hot dogs. So good. They talked recipes and cooking techniques until they had finished cleaning up. They hopped on the four-wheeler and went to the lake for a campfire. They shared a bottle of wine and played "I have never, ever..." and laughed and laughed at some of the crazy things they came up with, being very careful not to get too personal.

"Let me ask you something," Davey said. "How do you get a name like MacKenzie Rose O'Riley? MacKenzie is clearly Scottish, and with your and your mom's red hair, it's a given. Then you have O'Riley, which is Irish with your dad. Explain your heritage, lass," he said in a bad Scottish brogue.

MacKenzie laughed. "I know, right? Well, you're right. My mother is Scottish, and her last name was MacKenzie—hence, my first name. Rose was my father's mother's name. Rose O'Riley. My father's family is from Dublin. And if you know anything about history, the Scots and the Irish don't exactly get along. My mother's family forbid her to marry my father, saying that 'the damn Irish lad won't amount to anything,'" Mackenzie said in a perfect Scottish accent. "Well, my parents eloped, and they obviously had the last laugh about the prophecy of my mother's future with the Scotsman ...well, the General. In time, the families came together, but they have all passed away now. I wish I could talk to my ancestors about the countries of my origin. So much knowledge gone," she said, smiling dreamily. "My father still calls me his bonny lass."

"I think your ancestors would have been extremely proud of their granddaughter," Davey said.

MacKenzie's eyes teared up. Silly being emotional about people she had never even met.

"And your dad's right. You are the bonniest lass who has ever been," Davey said quietly.

MacKenzie wiped away a tear and stood up to poke the fire. "Like you've known many lasses," she laughed, trying to hide her emotions.

Davey remained seated and, so quietly that it almost couldn't be heard, "Lass or not, you're above them all," he said.

MacKenzie shifted uncomfortably. "How about we go up to the house? The sun really did me in today. I'm beat." She yawned.

There was an uncomfortable silence between them when they got back to the house. Davey told her she could sleep in his bed, and he would take one of his brother's beds. "Would you like another glass of wine before bed?" he asked.

MacKenzie shook her head. "No, I'm just going to go to bed. I will be ready by six tomorrow."

Davey poured himself another glass of wine. "Yeah. That will be fine. Do you need me to set my alarm?"

MacKenzie walked toward his room. "No, I'm all set. Good night, Davey." She closed the bedroom door.

Davey downed the wine. It was going to be a long night with her so close yet so far away.

19

Two weeks had passed since they came back from Maine. MacKenzie had thought being around Davey at work would get easier with time and she wouldn't want to cry in her tea every night, but she was wrong. She was so conflicted. On one hand, she desperately wanted to be around him, but at the same time, it broke her heart that they couldn't be really together. A little voice in her head kept repeating that if she just gave in and went to him, at least they could be together for a short time. The only thing stopping her was the knowledge that, if she did that, she would never be the same. Her love would grow so strong that when he decided to end the relationship, she might not survive it. The thought of her becoming this desperate, pathetic woman begging him not to leave her terrified her enough to not even entertain the idea of "playing this out," as he had put it.

It was late, and MacKenzie was reading in bed when there was a knock at her door. Instantly afraid, she quietly made her way to the door to look through the peephole. Davey stood outside her door, looking disheveled and nervous. Without thinking, MacKenzie opened the door, not realizing she was only wearing one of Roberto's old soccer shirts with his name, Savoy, on the back.

"Davey, what is it? Is something wrong?" MacKenzie asked, concerned.

Davey just stared at her with his hands in his pockets. He shook his head as he took in her bare legs and feet. "Um, yeah. I'm sorry it's so late, but I wanted to tell you in person. My brothers and I are going to where Jack is modeling tomorrow to try to see her. I won't be at work," he said, walking through the door.

"Davey, that's wonderful! I'm so happy for you!" she said, hugging him before she realized what she was doing. She started to pull back, but he held her tight.

"I miss you, MacKenzie," Davey whispered in her hair.

MacKenzie closed her eyes and let herself smell and feel him before slowly pulling out of his embrace. "Um, can I get you something to drink?" she asked shyly, feeling uncomfortable in just her T-shirt.

Davey shook his head. "No, I don't want to keep you up. I just wanted to let you know what was happening. Do you mind if I tell Jack that you work at the restaurant?" he asked.

"Oh, Davey, I would rather you didn't say anything right now. If you do make contact, I think I will wait a while to seek her out."

Davey nodded. "I don't necessarily agree, but I will respect your decision for now," he said, walking toward the door.

"Thank you," MacKenzie said, leaning on the open door.

Davey leaned over and kissed her forehead. "Sleep well, sweetheart," he said, walking down the hall.

"Night," MacKenzie said quietly. She closed her door, locked it, then leaned against it and tried to calm her erratic pulse. The pain was real. A real physical ache in the pit of her stomach. Would it ever get easier to be around him?

The next day MacKenzie was on pins and needles, wondering what was happening with Davey. To make her mind stop racing, she decided to make a dessert that reminded her of her best friend, Jack. Maine whoopie pies were Jack's favorite treat—two decadent chocolate cakes held together with loads of sugary white frosting. I think the customers will enjoy them, she thought, heading out to the Corner Market for extra ingredients.

The whoopie pies were a huge hit. Before she left for the evening, she wrapped up four of them to bring to Ink. Trina had called her for an impromptu game of dirty Scrabble.

The treats were a big hit at Ink. It was really nice to see her friends, and she won the game, using all her tiles to spell *buttplug*. To say the crew was impressed would be an understatement. As everyone was laughing and high fiving her, she heard her phone ring. She answered it but was unable to hear above the rowdy crew. "Hello?" she said for the second time, plugging her other ear to hear better.

"MacKenzie!" Davey hollered through the phone.

MacKenzie jumped up and went out to the sidewalk so she could hear. "Davey?" she asked.

"Where the fuck are you? I've called you three times, but the calls went to voice mail, and it sounds like you're at a bar," he said crossly.

MacKenzie stiffened. "I'm visiting friends. How did it go today with Jack?" she asked, trying to change the subject.

There was a pause. "Are you in SoHo, MacKenzie? Have you been drinking?" he asked.

MacKenzie sighed. "Davey, you're not the General. Yes, I'm in SoHo, and no, I haven't been drinking. Now are you going to tell me how today went?"

"It was good, real good. We saw her and went to her brownstone here in New York. It was nice to all be together again—well, except for my father. I'll tell you more tomorrow, although there isn't all that much to tell. I just wanted to let you know that much. That's what friends do, isn't it, MacKenzie?" he asked, leaving a lump in her throat.

"Um, yes, and I appreciate you calling. I'll see you tomorrow, Davey," she said.

"Oh, wait, MacKenzie?"

"Yes?"

"You can just delete the three messages I left. I was worried about you," he said and hung up.

MacKenzie frowned and dialed her voice mail. All three messages were him yelling "Where the fuck are you?" into the phone. "He definitely needs a better bedside manner," she mumbled as she walked back into the tattoo parlor.

"Hey, sweetheart, is everything OK?" Z asked.

Mackenzie smiled and nodded.

"Come on, you can tell us. It's that man, isn't it?" Z looked intently at MacKenzie.

MacKenzie sat back on the couch and pressed her fingers to her temples. "God, is it that obvious?" she grimaced.

Trina and Z laughed. "Um, yeah, but we've all been there, lassie," Trina said.

"Well, I have some news that might cheer you up," Z said brightly. MacKenzie looked interested. "I have this lady who comes in for tats with me. She's a librarian. Well, she was telling me that she was starting a book club based on the books and television show *Outlander*. She wanted to know if I knew anybody who might be interested, and I immediately thought of you, sweet thing."

MacKenzie completely sucked up all the air in the room. "What? Am I interested? I think I would marry this woman. Yes, yes, I am very interested," she said, laughing.

Z laughed, too. "I thought so, and it will be good for you to meet new people. I'll get the contact info she gave me," she said, going to her office. MacKenzie stood up when Z came back into the room. "Here ya go, sweet pea. Feel free to let your geek flag fly."

MacKenzie laughed and hugged her. "Oh, it will be flying high! Thanks again for thinking of me. It means a lot. I've got to go. It's a school night, you know." She hugged everybody before she left for the subway.

20

At work Monday afternoon, MacKenzie sat in the break room and dialed Penny's number. When Penny picked up, MacKenzie told her that Z had given her the number. Penny knew who she was immediately, and they talked like they had been friends for some time. Penny indicated that besides her and MacKenzie, there were four other members of the book club. Penny asked if this Saturday night was good for MacKenzie, and MacKenzie indicated that indeed Saturday night was fine. Penny gave her her address in SoHo and said she would see her then.

As MacKenzie was confirming the address and time with Penny, Davey came into the break room and leaned against the counter. MacKenzie hung up and looked at Davey. "Did you need something?"

Davey crossed his arms on his chest. "Um, I just wanted to know if you would like to come over to my place tonight, and I can fill you in on what I know about Jack," he said.

MacKenzie stood up and looked at him. "We could just go into your office, and you could tell me."

Davey took a step closer to MacKenzie, leaning down to whisper in her ear. "We could, but I want your time and attention. I miss you, MacKenzie. Please."

All her resolve left her. She smelled him, wanted him, and desperately missed him. She closed her eyes and nodded. "Yes," she said quietly.

"Great. We'll leave here at nine," he whispered with his nose in her hair.

MacKenzie nodded, walked back to the kitchen, and put her earbuds in with shaking hands to continue work.

All afternoon, Davey worked around the kitchen and kept stealing glances at MacKenzie as she worked her magic in the form of *tres leches* bread pudding with vanilla cream sauce. She was truly amazing. He battled with himself as he worked. He knew he couldn't offer her what she wanted and deserved, but he still couldn't stay away from her. It was a physical ache that he felt, and the need to touch her was all-consuming. Along with the ache for her, there was jealousy swirling around in there as well. Did she have a date on Saturday night? Is that what he had walked in on, her making plans? And what kind of loser made her go to his apartment in SoHo? And another thing, whose soccer T-shirt was she wearing the other night? Her loser ex-boyfriend? Jesus, he was driving himself nuts. He would finish prep and then go for a run.

MacKenzie was so absorbed in her work that she never saw Davey leave for a run. Seeing movement out of the corner of eye made her look up as Davey walked through the kitchen toward his office with no shirt and just his running shorts on. Sweat covered his broad chest, making his skin gleam. MacKenzie froze as their eyes locked. Davey stopped dead in his tracks. MacKenzie's eyes dropped to his chest and his glistening biceps.

All at once, Davey pulled her earbud out of her ear. "Stop looking at me like that, MacKenzie Rose, or I'm going to take you to my office, bend you over my desk, and fuck you," he whispered roughly in her ear.

Mackenzie's face turned red. "Stop it, Davey," she hissed.

"I can't. You're all I think about. Why do you think I need to go on so many runs? I'm trying to run away from you, but it seems to be a losing battle. I'm going to go shower. Feel free to join me if you'd like," he said with a smirk as he walked away.

MacKenzie took a deep breath and put her earbud back in. "Insufferable beast," she muttered to herself. Her heart was thundering in her chest, and all she wanted to do was walk back there and get in that shower. She closed her eyes and moaned. The want and need were increasing every day. What was she going to do?

As they rode to Davey's apartment, he told her what a hit her dessert had been that night. On any other occasion, MacKenzie would have been over the moon, but tonight, she was acutely aware of Davey's nearness, the small brush of touch as he helped her into the car, and his side glances at her as he drove. She still hadn't quite recovered from his comment about bending her over his desk. Sweet Jesus, she wanted to be bent over his desk! OK focus, they were going to talk about Jack and just spend time together like friends do. She never wanted to climb any of her other friends, though. Focus. Focus.

Davey's apartment was amazing. Everything was white and chrome with splashes of color from gorgeous paintings scattered throughout. "Oh, Davey, it's beautiful!" MacKenzie said, walking around. She picked up photos from around the apartment and smiled as she remembered each of the family members. MacKenzie gasped as she spied a snapshot of herself and Jack laughing on a blanket in the park. She smiled as she picked up the photo. "I remember that day. It was the picnic in the park," she said.

Davey came over and stood close to MacKenzie. "It's one of my favorite photos. You both look so happy. MacKenzie, I only want to see you happy." He touched a piece of her hair.

MacKenzie took a deep breath and put the photo back down. "Um, tell me about your meeting with Jack," she said, refocusing the conversation.

Davey stood looking at her thoughtfully, nodded and sighed, and then walked to the kitchen. "She looked amazing as you can imagine, being a supermodel and all," he said, pouring two glasses of red wine and handing her one. "But aside from that, she laid down some conditions for staying in contact with her. We cannot ask her about what she went through at all. She just said she's not the same girl who left that day, and she will never speak about it with us. She doesn't want us to pressure her to see Dad. When and if she is ready to have contact with him, then she will let us know," Davey said, looking sad.

MacKenzie's heart sank. "But, Davey, that's a good start," she said encouragingly, touching his arm. Davey sighed, put his head back, and closed his eyes. "Davey, what is it? Tell me."

Davey lifted his head and looked at her. He had tears in his eyes. "I saw the hurt in her eyes, MacKenzie. She said she didn't blame us at all, but it still kills me that we, her brothers, weren't there to protect her when she needed us. That's our job, and we failed."

MacKenzie threw her arms around him. "Davey, you can only go forward from here. You can't dwell on the past. Be happy she's back in your life. You guys are the best brothers ever."

Davey tightened his arms around her and buried his face in her neck, drinking in her scent and feel. "MacKenzie, I don't want to hurt you," he whispered against her neck as he began kissing behind her ear.

MacKenzie took a big gulp of air and shivered. "Davey," she whispered in need. Davey lifted his head and embraced her face, gently looking her in the eyes.

"Tell me to stop, MacKenzie, and I will. Tell me now," he pleaded.

MacKenzie looked into his eyes. "I can't," she whispered.

Davey moaned and took her mouth in an urgent kiss, his tongue tasting her mouth and sucking at her tongue. MacKenzie moaned and pressed her body against him as much as was possible. She felt his need against her belly. She kissed him back desperately. Davey's shaking fingers unbuttoned her white work blouse and tossed it on the floor. MacKenzie was frantically unbuttoning his white dress shirt as well and tossed it to the floor. She lifted his undershirt over his head and ran her fingers lightly over his chest, followed by her lips.

Davey let his head fall back and he grasped her hips and ground himself against her. MacKenzie pulled away and kneeled as she kissed down his stomach and took hold of his belt to unfasten it. Davey's head shot up and he looked down at her with need in his eyes. MacKenzie held his eye contact as she unfastened his belt and unbuttoned his pants. She pulled the zipper down very slowly. "Jesus, you're killing me, MacKenzie," he moaned.

MacKenzie pulled his pants down along with his boxers to find him gloriously hard and ready for her mouth. She touched him lightly with her tongue. He moaned as she put him in her mouth. MacKenzie still looked at him as she took all of him to the back of her throat. She repeated that over and over as one hand held his buttocks and the other stroked his manhood as she sucked. Davey's hand went to her hair to pull her deeper onto him. He was close as he lifted her in one swift movement and started walking toward his bedroom. "Jesus, fuck, MacKenzie, you're going to kill me," he said, setting her down in his dark bedroom.

Davey turned on the bedside light and kissed her. "Stay with me tonight, please," he said as he unfastened her bra and let it fall to the floor. Davey bent, took her breast into his mouth, and gently sucked. MacKenzie moaned and thought her knees would buckle. "Answer me, MacKenzie," he said letting his tongue flick her tight nub.

MacKenzie drew a quick breath. "Yes, yes," she said breathlessly.

"Tell me what you want, MacKenzie," Davey said, kissing her lips as he unbuttoned her black slacks and put his hand inside her panties to gently stroke her. He put his other arm around her and pushed her feet apart with his foot. "Tell me," he said against her lips as he inserted two fingers into her, and she moaned.

"Touch me, taste me," she said moaning.

He worked his fingers in and out of her. "Is that all you want me to do, MacKenzie? Are you sure?" he asked, finding her clit and stroking and gently squeezing.

MacKenzie cried out, holding herself up by winding her arms around his neck. "You. I want you to fuck me, Davey," she said into his neck.

"Jesus," he moaned. He pushed her gently back on the bed and grasped her panties and slacks and pulled them off her. Dear God, she was gorgeous. He laid her out and began kissing her neck and then down to her breast slowly sucking and licking one breast and then the other. MacKenzie was gripping his hair and bowed up on the bed in need.

"I'm going to take my time with you, MacKenzie. You're going to lose count of how many times you come. I crave you like a drug, MacKenzie Rose. What have you done to me?" he said, kissing his way down her flat belly to the apex between her legs.

Davey spread her legs and looked at her glistening sex. "You are so fucking beautiful," he said as he began to devour her. MacKenzie's hips shot off the bed, and she screamed. Davey grasped her hips and pulled them down, anchoring her. MacKenzie's hands gripped his silky hair tightly. She rode his mouth until she arched her back and cried out in orgasm. Davey never let up but continued to taste her. He added two fingers along with his mouth, and before long MacKenzie cried out again as she shattered. Davey waited until her spasms subsided as he kissed her sex gently and crawled up her body to hover over her. He kissed her deeply, letting her taste her sweetness. "I need to be inside you, sweetheart. What do you need? What do you want?" he asked urgently.

MacKenzie looked shy. "Can I lean over the bed, and you love me from behind?" she whispered.

Davey put his forehead on hers. "Jesus, yes," he said, moving off the bed and turning her around.

MacKenzie bent over the bed. Davey used his hand at the back of her neck to gently force her farther down on the bed so her forehead rested on the bed and her arms were on either side of her head. Davey angled himself at her entrance just before he drove into her in one swift stroke. MacKenzie cried out. There was slight pain but mostly just being filled so completely and deeply.

Davey stilled. "Are you OK, sweetheart?" he asked with tension in his voice. It took all the willpower he possessed to not move inside her. Sweet Jesus, she was so tight and warm.

"Oh, don't stop, please. You're so deep. I've never felt anything like it," she said urgently.

Davey growled, grabbed her by the hips, and began driving into her hard and fast. He wasn't going to last. Not with his pent-up need for her and her tight sex clenching him like a fist. Davey reached around and hugged her close and with his other hand found her clit, and MacKenzie screamed and fell off the precipice in another orgasm. As soon as MacKenzie started to orgasm, her sex grabbed his manhood, and he let himself holler and release the most intense orgasm he had ever experienced.

Gasping for breath, he lay his face on her back before embracing her and falling on the bed with her in his arms. She turned around and laid her head on his chest, trying to catch her breath. As their breathing returned to normal, the rhythmic rise and fall of his chest put her fast asleep. Davey stroked her hair, knowing she had fallen asleep. It was probably for the best because he had no fucking idea what was happening. He had never experienced a need so great in his life. He would trade almost anything for more of what he just experienced with MacKenzie. It was so much more than lust. He had felt intense lust before, and this was much bigger than that. This was love. This was something that could bring him to his knees.

This had to stop. MacKenzie deserved more than he was willing to give her. It made him angry at himself for cheapening her to accept what he offered. She deserved a long life with a loving husband and lots of little red-haired babies. The thought of MacKenzie holding a little baby with red wispy hair made him smile. She would be a great mother. Thinking of MacKenzie mothering another man's baby had his guts twisting. God, he didn't think he would be strong enough to stand by and watch that. The only answer was to end it before he let it destroy him, he thought as he drifted off to sleep with MacKenzie tangled around him.

— ~

MacKenzie woke with a start and lifted her head off Davey's chest. Shit. It took a few minutes to adjust to her surroundings. She had fallen asleep after they made love. Had sex. Might as well call it what it was to him. She watched him sleep for a few minutes, taking in his mussed-up hair and his dark two-day beard growth. He was the most handsome man she had ever laid eyes on. He looked so peaceful resting there. She didn't think she would ever feel peace again. She had to leave before he woke up and things got awkward. She sighed and gently eased off the bed. She found her clothes. This was her first walk of shame. Although she wasn't actually going straight to work but home to shower, she still felt shameful. What must he think of her? She had practically begged him to love her. She was pathetic. She needed to get a grip and move on with her life. Starting today, she would put herself out there. Eventually, the pain of not having his love would ease, and maybe she could love someone else. She didn't know if she could do that. After all, she had loved Davey since she was seventeen years old. Pathetic, she thought as she made her way out of his apartment and walked toward a cab at the curb.

The rest of the week Davey and MacKenzie avoided each other like the plague: Davey because he was so angry at MacKenzie for sneaking out without saying goodbye and MacKenzie because she just didn't know what to say so she said nothing. Saturday came, and the kitchen was quiet. Every time Davey walked through, Luis just glared at him. MacKenzie plugged in her earbuds and focused on her work. She planned to finish early so she could make it to her first book club meeting. She was pretty excited about the group. She had read what the other group members were reading and was more than excited to see what their thoughts were about Jamie and Claire from *Outlander*.

MacKenzie walked back to Davey's office to find him behind his desk. She knocked lightly. He looked up. "Come in. You don't need to knock, MacKenzie. What do you need?" he asked, sitting back in his office chair. MacKenzie stood behind the chair in front of his desk with her duffel bag on her shoulder.

"Um, my work is done, and the rush is over. Do you mind if I take off?" she asked.

Davey looked at his watch. "No, of course not. You always stay later than you need to."

MacKenzie nodded and smiled. "Great. I'm just going to change. I'll see you Monday," she said turning to leave.

"Wait. Change in my bathroom. It's bigger," he said, motioning to his adjoining bathroom.

MacKenzie shook her head. "No, it's fine. I'll—"

"MacKenzie, just change in this bathroom. Don't make everything so difficult," he said angrily.

MacKenzie squared her shoulders in anger and marched into the bathroom. She changed into a red Indian print maxi dress with spaghetti straps. She slipped on a pair of strappy sandals, let her hair down, and fluffed it up, and she was ready. She walked out of the bathroom to Davey sitting on the edge of his desk with his keys in his hand.

He looked her up and down. Oh, fuck, no, was she going to SoHo looking like that! She put her head down and tried to edge past him.

Davey stood up. "I'll drive you," he said firmly.

MacKenzie stopped and stared at him, stunned. "No," she said, shaking her head.

He lifted her duffel bag from her shoulder. "I wasn't asking permission, MacKenzie. I'm driving you," he said, walking through the kitchen and out onto the sidewalk. "If your date can't pick you up, then I will bring you and pick you up so you're not riding the subway at night. Again, not up for discussion." He walked toward his car.

"Date?" MacKenzie asked. "I don't have a date. I'm going to a book club meeting." She stopped and crossed her arms over her chest.

Davey threw her duffel bag in the back seat and walked back to her. "Is that what they're calling it now?" he asked as she inhaled.

"It is a book club. I just joined. Not that I have to explain myself to you, anyway," she said, glaring at him.

Anger flashed in his eyes. "No, you don't even have the common courtesy to say goodbye. You just sneak out in the middle of the night," he snarled at her.

MacKenzie looked shocked. "What do you care? I saved you from the awkwardness of the light of day," she spat at him.

"There have been a lot of things between us, MacKenzie, but never awkwardness," he said, a little of the heat dissipating. "Look, I have to go to SoHo anyway tonight, so I might as well drop you off and pick you up," he said with finality.

MacKenzie took a deep breath. Shed feel like a child if she refused, so she nodded. He might bring her, but she would make sure she took a cab home. Bur he didn't have to know that.

Davey opened the passenger side door and helped her into the car. He got in the driver's side and started the engine. "You look beautiful tonight," he said grudgingly.

MacKenzie turned to look at him, staring straight ahead, driving. She shook her head. He was so confusing.

"Thank you," she said, looking out the window. They didn't speak until they got to SoHo, and he asked her the address. When he pulled up to the curb, he asked the apartment number. MacKenzie just looked at him. "Twenty-four. You know, the General never asked this many questions," she muttered as she got out of the car and opened the back door to retrieve her duffel bag.

"Just leave that since I'm picking you up. I'll wait for your call," he said.

That call is never going to come, she thought grimly as she grabbed her purse. "Fine. Thank you for the ride," she said. She closed the car door and walked inside the apartment complex.

MacKenzie hadn't had so much fun in a long time. Penny, the host and librarian that Z knew, was an absolute delight. With long black hair, she looked like she'd just stepped out of a gypsy movie. Sherry, a computer worker and mother of three, looked a little harassed but thankful for the evening to herself. Jo was a single waitress about thirty years old. Molly was an overworked social worker, married with no children. Last and most surprising was Dez, a rugged construction worker. The wine flowed. They all told a little bit about themselves and found themselves laughing and very comfortable with each other.

They had been discussing the book for about an hour when the doorbell rang. Penny answered it and walked back into the living room with Davey right behind her. MacKenzie was speechless. She just stared. Penny smiled. "Everyone, this is Dave, and he belongs to MacKenzie." Everyone shook his hand and introduced themselves.

MacKenzie still just stared as Davey sat beside her on the sofa. "Don't mind me, really, just continue with your discussion like I'm not even here."

MacKenzie shook her head, and before long she was deeply engaged in the battle of Culloden. Sherry was the first to yawn and stand up to leave, which prompted all of them to say their good nights.

With his hand on the small of her back, Davey guided MacKenzie to the car. They drove for a few minutes in silence before MacKenzie turned to him with her anger bubbling over. "What the hell was that, Davey Johnson?" she said in a low angry tone.

He looked over at her. "What are you talking about? Oh, you mean showing up early to your book club because I knew you had no intention of calling me to pick you up? Is that what you mean, MacKenzie?"

MacKenzie glared at him. How had he known she had no intention of calling him? "What about telling them you belong to me?" she asked.

Davey shrugged. "Those were Penny's words, not mine. But either way, it's true, MacKenzie. I do belong to you," he said quietly and looked over at her.

MacKenzie lost her breath for a moment and stared out the passenger window. What does that even mean? Her heart couldn't take much more of this. When they pulled up to the curb, MacKenzie started to open the door.

Davey put his hand on her arm. "Would you please wait for me to open the door for you? You can't tell me the General didn't open the door for your mom?" Davey got out of the car, opened her door, and helped her out.

"You're not the General, Davey. Is that what you want, to be my father?" she asked as he grabbed her duffel bag.

He got very close to her face. "No, I most certainly don't want to be your father, MacKenzie Rose," he said, propelling her toward the building entrance. They reached her door, and Davey put her duffel bag down beside her. "Well, good night. Sleep well. I'll see you on Monday at the market." He turned to leave.

"Davey, thank you for the ride. I do appreciate it," she said frustrated.

"You're welcome, and MacKenzie, for the record, I don't like that there is a man in your book club."

MacKenzie rolled her eyes. "Oh, for goodness' sake! Good night, Davey," she said and walked into her apartment.

21

Work was a blessing and a curse to MacKenzie. A blessing because it kept her mind occupied and not dwelling on what she couldn't have with Davey. A curse because she had to see and interact with said Davey every workday. Most days the happy/sad meter was off the charts.

It had been crazy busy at the restaurant. MacKenzie was busy making a special order of cupcakes for a family coming in the next day to celebrate their little girl's birthday. How could she not make the cupcakes for the family? She was just finishing up frosting them when she heard her name called. She looked up to see Jack standing there.

MacKenzie's heart flip-flopped, and she immediately started crying. She ran to embrace her very best friend. Oh, how she had missed her girlfriend. MacKenzie hadn't seen Jack since that summer four years ago when her father had sent her away. Jack had run away from the halfway house she had been sent to, and her brothers and father had been searching for her until recently, when she was discovered in Paris. MacKenzie had begged the General to help in the search as well. There wasn't much MacKenzie wouldn't do for her summer sister.

They went out back to Davey's office and talked for a while. Jack was indeed changed because of what she had gone through, but in all ways that mattered, she was the same tough-as-nails, smart-mouthed girl MacKenzie had loved. They both wanted to know everything that had happened in each others lives since they they'd last seen each other so they decided to have a sleepover at MacKenzie's apartment. They talked and laughed well into the night before falling asleep.

MacKenzie felt Jack shaking her roughly awake. "Hey, Mac attack, wake up! How would you like to spend four glorious days in sunny Mexico?" Jack asked her, using one of many nicknames she had for MacKenzie.

"What? What are you talking about?" MacKenzie watched Jack dial and speak to Davey. MacKenzie was wide awake now and listening to the exchange between Davey and Jack.

"Yes, Davey, the Worthington Jet will take us to Mexico and we will have plenty of security. I'm going there for WORK but Mac and I will have some time together too. Much needed time I might add."

Jack handed the phone to MacKenzie. "Yes?" MacKenzie asked into the phone.

"MacKenzie, do you want to go with Jack?" Davey asked.

"Yes," she replied.

"Will you please be careful and not get into any trouble?" he asked. MacKenzie sighed. "Of course."

"One more thing, MacKenzie," he said softly.

"Yes?" MacKenzie asked.

"I'll miss you," he said. MacKenzie's heart stopped. Why did he confuse her so?

"Bye, Davey," she whispered and handed the phone back to Jack.

The private jet that took them to Mexico was amazing. MacKenzie had never seen such opulence. The bathroom alone was almost the size of her entire apartment. As they ate their breakfast, MacKenzie asked Jack about Jared. MacKenzie had read the recent article about his gaming company. Jack and Jared were meant to be together. Jack broke down and told her about that night getting caught by her father. Jack had no idea why Jared never came to get her and had grieved about it ever since. Jack's heartbreak was as fresh as it had been that summer night four years ago. MacKenzie decided to let the subject drop, and instead, they watched movies until they landed.

Mexico was glorious. While Jack worked in the afternoons, MacKenzie sat by the pool and read *Outlander* for her book club. More than one hopeful male guest tried to make conversation with her, but her heart simply wasn't in it. Her heart belonged completely to another.

Jack and MacKenzie had been able to catch up with each other's lives like they had not missed the last four years.

On the last evening, the two decided to hire a car to take them into the town for dinner and dancing. After sharing a bottle of wine with dinner, they danced until around midnight before deciding to call it a night. Jack wanted to walk on the beach before they headed back, so the two walked out onto the dark beach illuminated by a full moon. They hadn't walked far up the beach before they found themselves surrounded by three local men who clearly had bad intentions.

Jack told MacKenzie to run back to the restaurant and wait for her. MacKenzie ran about halfway before she turned to watch Jack break two of the men's noses. MacKenzie screamed as she saw the other lunge at Jack with a knife. Jack was cut and screamed for MacKenzie to run and wait for her. MacKenzie did as she was told but waited in the doorway until Jack came running toward her.

She was hurt badly. MacKenzie helped her into a taxi and took her phone. Jack told MacKenzie to call Sam, who was number one in Jack's contacts. Jack reassured Mac that he would know what to do; she felt like she was going to pass out. Sam was calm and gave MacKenzie instructions to get Jack back to the hotel room. He said he would send someone to help Jack.

When MacKenzie had finally gotten Jack back to the hotel room and they were waiting for the doctor, Sam called back and asked MacKenzie how she knew Jack. MacKenzie told Sam about the summer they became friends. Sam explained that he ran the soup kitchen, and that was how he had first met Jack. He said she was like the daughter he never had. The doctor arrived and patched Jack up. Sam stayed on the line with MacKenzie. When the doctor left, Sam told MacKenzie that Jack would sleep, and she should as well. MacKenzie curled up on the bed beside Jack. She cried for the fighter that Jack had had to become; she cried for her broken heart; she just cried.

〜 〜

Davey picked them up at the airport, but he didn't seem happy. He barely spoke to MacKenzie in the car and tried to interrogate Jack until she told him about some vulgar sex that the two of them had engaged in. After they dropped Jack off, Davey didn't speak to MacKenzie until they reached her apartment. Davey turned to her in the seat. "So tell me what happened," he said angrily.

MacKenzie turned toward him, surprised that he might know something. She had promised Jack that she wouldn't say a word. "I don't know what you're talking about. We had a lovely time together," she said looking him in the eye.

Davey shook his head and hit the steering wheel hard. "Damn it, MacKenzie! I know something happened. Neither one of you answered your phones last night, and you both look like hell today," he said harshly.

"Davey, we're fine. I'm fine. I will get changed and come to work. Do you want to wait for me?" she asked, getting out of the car.

Davey bolted out of the car. "For Christ's sake, how many times do I have to ask you to wait for me to open your door?" He grabbed the door and offered her his hand.

MacKenzie took his hand, confused. "I'm sorry," she said distractedly.

Davey got her duffel bag and walked her to her door. "I want you to lie down and rest. Come into work tomorrow after a good night's sleep." He dropped her duffel bag at her feet, gathered her close, and hugged her. "I really missed you," he whispered in her ear.

All the pent-up emotions from the last twenty-four hours caught up with her, and she hugged him tight. "I missed you, too," she whispered brokenly.

Davey heard her voice crack and pulled back to look at her. "Whoa, hey, what's wrong, sweetheart?" he asked, seeing her tears.

MacKenzie tried to brush them away, but they just kept falling. "I need you, Davey. I don't want to be alone right now. Can you just come in and lie with me until I fall asleep?" she asked.

Davey took the key from Mackenzie's hands, unlocked the door, pulled her inside, and walked her to her bed. He slowly undressed her until she stood before him in only her panties. He saw her old boyfriend's T-shirt that she wore to bed, picked it up, and threw it across the room. He pulled down the covers on the bed, and she climbed in. Davey lay down and drew her into his arms.

MacKenzie sighed. She felt safe. Even as her heart broke being with him, she simply couldn't stand the thought of not being able to see him and touch him. She drifted off to sleep as Davey gently stroked her hair.

Something had happened, Davey was certain, but he also knew that the two of them were thick as thieves and wouldn't tell on each other. He sighed. He had known as soon MacKenzie had stepped off the plane that something was off. How was it possible that he was so in tune with MacKenzie? What was it about her that made him want to protect her and murder anyone who threatened to hurt her or take her away from him? He knew he had no right to these feelings, but he had them just the same. He also knew how confusing this all was for her, but for fuck sakes, he didn't understand any of it either. He gently got up and scribbled a note that he would be back later to check on her and would bring dinner with him.

At nine o'clock, a knock sounded at the door. MacKenzie was glad she had taken the time to rest and shower. She had taken extra care with her hair and make-up, thrown on a simple summer dress, and stayed barefoot. She opened the door to Davey, holding a large bag that smelled delicious. MacKenzie moaned. "That smells like my favorite, beef stroganoff," she said.

Davey smiled as he came in and set the bag on the counter. "You would be correct. Now sit down, and let me serve you," he said, holding out a chair for her. Before she sat down, he put his arm around her and brought her close. "You look beautiful," he said and kissed her. He ended the kiss, and she sat down.

She couldn't help but moan throughout the meal. When he looked up from his plate in pain, MacKenzie laughed. "I'm sorry, but I can't help it. I love how you make this. It's my favorite. Thank you for making it." She took another bite and moaned again.

Davey put his fork down and came around the table. He hauled her up and kissed her deeply. "Jesus, do you have any idea what you do to me?" he growled. He pulled her dress over her head to find her naked. "Holy fuck!" he said. He took her breast into his mouth and sucked. Mackenzie's legs buckled as she moaned. He caught her and carried her to the bed. He set her down and quickly undressed. Naked, he stretched out beside her and stroked her breast, moving his hand slowly down to her glistening sex. He stroked a finger along her cleft to find her wet and ready. He kissed her deeply. "I need to be inside you, MacKenzie," he said, situating himself over her at her entrance.

MacKenzie spread her legs wide. "Yes, please, Davey. I need you," she said urgently.

That was all the encouragement he needed. He plunged deep inside her and moaned at the euphoria that overtook him. He had never felt anything like this in his life. It was as if his very soul was participating in the act. There was something different about this encounter. He couldn't take his time and pleasure her before he entered her. The need to be inside her, and the need to claim her overwhelmed him.

MacKenzie kissed and nipped at his neck, making him crazy. He thrust in and out of her like a madman. He lifted up and grasped her head in his hands. "Look at me, MacKenzie. You make me fucking crazy!" he said in an urgent whisper.

MacKenzie's eyes got big, and she gasped. "Davey! Oh, Jesus, please, more, harder, oh, I love you!" she said, completely shattering into a million pieces. Davey couldn't hold back any longer. He lifted her legs high and thrust hard and fast into her, following her into the abyss. He rolled off her and pulled her to him as they let their breathing return to normal.

Did she actually say that out loud? She was pretty sure she did, and she just wanted to jump out her apartment window. Just when she was about to say something, Davey spoke up and made the decision for both of them.

"You realize that the grand opening of *Harmony* is next weekend, right? It's going to be crazy busy getting ready this week," he said.

OK...so I guess we'll just pretend that outburst never happened. Good, denial is good, right? MacKenzie's eyes were heavy, and she let herself drift off to sleep.

Davey held MacKenzie, letting himself adjust to the knowledge that she loved him. He had this sick feeling in his stomach. It was a mix of joy and terror. Was this what love felt like? He knew it was. He had just been fooling himself that she hadn't burrowed her way into his heart. It still didn't change anything, though. He wouldn't offer her more than what they had. If she would only give in and let them play out whatever this was, they could both move on with their lives.

Why couldn't she see how inevitable it was? They could hardly stand to be in each other's company without having a sexual meltdown. That was it. He was going to try to make her see reason and have this affair. He had tried to stay away from her, but he couldn't, so now he would try to break her walls down. Didn't she see? The sooner they played this out, the sooner she could find Mr. Right and have the yard full of kids. Somehow, this thought made Davey want to throw up.

22

The evening of the grand opening, MacKenzie rushed home from the restaurant to shower and change. Jack came by to drop her dress and shoes off. She had gotten MacKenzie a dress from the new line of Worthing evening wear. It was truly spectacular. MacKenzie had never seen such a beautiful dress. It was a gorgeous emerald-green silk, formfitting and off the shoulder. Jack had included a pair of black high heels with red soles to wear. Everything fit like a glove. She didn't have time to do anything with her hair, but luckily, it had grown out, and there was enough curl so she could just pull it back with a white ribbon.

MacKenzie grabbed her shawl and raced out of her apartment to catch a cab. She was going to have just enough time to get back to the restaurant before the grand opening of *Harmony* began. The restaurant had been booked for quite some time. There would be entertainment, and everybody of any importance would be in attendance.

She was just looking over all the desserts when Davey walked out of his office and stopped short. MacKenzie looked up and, holy hell, he looked amazing in his black tux. Yum. His hair was combed, but he must have run his hands through it like he did absentmindedly, so it was just mussed up enough to look sexy as hell. When she found his eyes, she gasped at the heat she saw there. Instantly she felt hot and wet.

Davey's eyes drank her in hungrily. "MacKenzie, Jesus, you're breathtakingly gorgeous," he said, swallowing hard. MacKenzie smiled, and it lit up her entire face, making her more stunning if that was possible. Davey held out his hand, pulled her into his office, and closed the door. He pushed her up against it and took her lips urgently. His tongue danced with hers, and they both moaned.

"I don't want you to go into the dining room tonight, OK? You can just hang out here in my office. I will bring you a plate of food, I promise," he said, kissing her bare neck. MacKenzie giggled. The sound made his stomach flutter.

"OK, I will do that if you stay in here with me," she said, pushing her hips hard against his erection. Davey moaned. "Fuck, don't do that, or you really won't make it out there," he said, kissing her neck, not able to get enough of her scent. He took a deep breath and looked at his watch. "Shit, we have to go. Now once you make sure everything is set in the kitchen, you must come out to the table with the rest of us for the evening. Jack's orders," he said, grabbing one last kiss.

Davey left the office walking through the kitchen, and moments later, Jack burst through the doors. She looked beautiful as always. They each admired the other and then went into the dining room. As they made their way to the head table, MacKenzie heard her name spoken in broken Italian, coming from the bar. She turned to find Carlo Alberto, an Italian businessman she and Roberto had associated with. He had always been kind to her. MacKenzie told Jack she would see her at the table.

She walked over to Carlo and smiled as he embraced her and kissed each cheek. Carlo asked her in Italian how she was, and without even thinking, she lapsed into Italian as well. "I'm well, thank you," she said. He motioned to the bartender for a glass of red wine. MacKenzie wondered if he remembered that's what she drank or was just a good guesser. Carlo motioned to the bar stool, and she sat down.

"Are you in town for business?" she asked, taking a sip of wine.

"Yes, I am here in New York on business, but I have been asked to come here tonight to see you," he said smiling.

MacKenzie looked shocked. "Why? Did Roberto ask you to come and check up on me? I talk to Roberto from time to time; we are still friends. Tell me, is that the reason you are here tonight?" she asked.

Davey watched from the crow's nest above the bar as a man addressed MacKenzie while she was walking to the table with Jack. Instantly, jealously ripped through him as the man embraced and kissed her. His hands fisted as he watched the man buy her a glass of wine and smile at her like he knew her. Davey asked Jared who the man was. Jared could hardly take his eyes off Jack. "That's Carlo Alberto, an Italian businessman. He just sunk a ton of money in my stocks today," Jared said, looking right back at Jack.

Davey tried to get Jared to come downstairs, but he refused. He left Jared upstairs to make his way to the bar. As soon as Davey approached, he heard Carlo tell MacKenzie that Roberto was a fool. Davey wanted to punch this man, but instead, he put his hand on MacKenzie's back to say in the subtlest way that she was his. Wait, did he have any right to tell the world she was his? Fuck, no, but it didn't matter; she *was* his, and he'd be damned if he let this Italian put his hands on her again.

"Hi, do you mind letting me introduce you around? It seems everyone is eager to meet the new pastry chef," Davey said to MacKenzie.

MacKenzie looked surprised and stood. "Oh, that would be great. Um, Davey this is Carlo Alberto, he's an Italian businessman here in New York for work," she said.

"Ah, not all work," Carlo said in broken English.

MacKenzie blushed. "Carlo, this is Dave Johnson, the owner of Harmony and my boss." She smiled uncomfortably.

Davey shook Carlo's hand when what he really wanted to do was bounce his face off the bar. Then he turned and escorted her away. "Getting a little friendly, weren't you?" he asked in her ear.

MacKenzie gasped. "No. He was just saying hello to me." she said as low as she could.

Davey leaned in closer. "Just so you know, while we're together, I don't share," he growled.

MacKenzie glared at him and hissed back. "Well that's good because we're *not* together, so there's nothing for you to share." She went to sit beside Jack, as far away from Davey as she could get. As Davey glared after her, his eyes caught Marcus grinning at him. Marcus lifted his drink in toast as if he knew something very important. Shit. Was it that obvious how he felt about MacKenzie?

23

Davey and MacKenzie avoided each other as much as possible for the next two weeks. On Friday night, MacKenzie was busy working when Davey came through looking like he was going out. He was freshly showered and wore a suit and tie. He smelled delicious, and MacKenzie was instantly jealous beyond anything she had ever felt before. She felt it more strongly than when she had caught Roberto cheating. He had been speaking to her, but she hadn't heard a word he said. She shook her head.

"MacKenzie, you're all set for tomorrow night, right?" he asked.

"What? Tomorrow night?" she asked dumbly.

Davey looked surprised. "Jack's birthday party. The cake?" he asked.

"Oh, yes, everything is set," she said quietly.

"Well, OK, I'll see you tomorrow, then. Thank you for staying with Mike tonight. I appreciate it," he said, walking out of the kitchen.

MacKenzie just stood there for a moment before she picked up a fresh loaf of bread and threw it at the door that Davey just walked out of. The loaf thumped the door and fell to the floor. Luis, Gabe, and Mario stared at her, dumbfounded. Mario went to pick up the bread and mumbled that he would take it home with him. MacKenzie huffed and went back to work. She kept imagining Davey taking out some leggy blonde. Oh, he was just getting her back about her comment that they weren't together. But really, they weren't together. She had only stated the obvious.

MacKenzie felt sick to her stomach, and she realized that she wouldn't survive if she had to watch Davey parade around with other women. She knew she couldn't do it, and why would she want to do that to herself? She needed to think about a future that didn't have Davey in it, and that probably meant leaving his restaurant. She would think about it later tonight because God knew she wasn't going to get any sleep.

Davey rang the doorbell and tried to squelch the sick feeling that what he was doing was wrong. Fuck it! He was doing nothing wrong. MacKenzie was right. They weren't a couple, and they both needed to move forward. Helena opened the door to her extravagant apartment with chandeliers and over-the-top decor. Her long black hair hung straight and lifeless, her eyes had so much make-up that she actually looked like a racoon, and her red dress was so low cut and tight that he thought it might rip if she sat down. Fuck me, this was a huge mistake.

Helena smiled and ushered him into her apartment. "How are you, Dave? I wondered if you were ever going to call me after our last date. That was months and months ago," she purred and laid her hand on his lapel. He wanted to step back. What was wrong with him? The last time he saw Helena, they had had a good dinner and come back to her apartment. If his memory served him, she was quite adventurous in bed. The thought repulsed him.

What. The. Fuck? What had MacKenzie done to him? He started to sweat. "Look, Helena, I just wanted to come up here to tell you that something has come up at the restaurant that needs my attention. I have to leave. I'm sorry for the inconvenience." Before Helena could even utter a sound, Davey turned and walked out the door. As soon as he reached the sidewalk, he took a deep breath and pulled out his phone. "Hi, Bobby, you guys around tonight? I'll be right over," he said and hung up.

MacKenzie got up early and headed to the restaurant to make Jack's birthday cake before she started on her regular desserts. She had her earbuds in when Davey tapped her shoulder, almost scaring her to death. MacKenzie jumped and pulled out her earbuds. Davey held up his hands. "Sorry, sorry, I didn't mean to jump you. Why are you here so early?"

He looked like shit. His shirt and pants were wrinkled, his hair was sticking up all over his head, he hadn't shaved, and he had dark circles under his eyes. Must have been quite a night. MacKenzie began to seethe.

"I'm making a birthday cake before I get to my other work. I'd rather not be bothered," she said crisply and put her earbuds back in. Davey tapped her again. MacKenzie looked up with fire in her eyes.

"I'm going to go shower and then go out for breakfast. Would you like to join me?" he said, crossing his arms over his chest.

Still glaring, MacKenzie shook her head. "No, thank you," she said and put her earbuds back in.

Davey stood there with narrowed eyes. Yeah, he was so glad he had decided last night not to date anyone until he and MacKenzie had sorted out whatever the fuck was between them. He had never met a more stubborn woman. Even so, he had gotten so angry when his brothers kept peppering him with questions about her, especially Caleb. Little fucker, he better stay away from MacKenzie or Davey would beat the shit out of him. Man, he felt like shit. No one can shame you into drinking shots like your brothers, and now he was paying dearly. A shower and a greasy breakfast would be a good idea before he tried to talk to MacKenzie again.

— ◆ —

The party was a big hit. It was wonderful to see Jack surrounded by her friends and family. It would have been perfect if her father could have been there, thought MacKenzie. Jack's brothers were so much fun, and they flirted with her until Davey came over and glared at them. MacKenzie glared at Davey. She was still so angry that he had gone on a date that she couldn't see straight. Davey had tried to talk to her multiple times during the day, but she had just answered with one word and kept herself plugged into her music as she worked.

As the party began to slow down, MacKenzie had had enough. She needed to get away from Davey's presence. She just couldn't breathe. She had just gone back to the kitchen to grab her things when Davey showed up and blocked the door to the breakroom. "Excuse me," MacKenzie said, wanting to pass by him.

Davey stayed where he was. "No," he said flatly.

MacKenzie looked surprised. "What? I need to pass, Davey. I'm going home. I'm tired," she said with a sigh.

Some of the heat left his eyes. "I know you're tired, but I want to know what the fuck is wrong with you, and I want to know now!" he said.

MacKenzie squared her shoulders. "Nothing. There is nothing wrong. Now please just let me pass," she said quietly.

Davey crossed his arms. "No," he said.

MacKenzie let out a frustrated huff, threw her bag on the table, and turned around to face him with her hands on her hips. Jesus, she was a sight to behold with her hair wild, curled for the party, her simple black wrap dress that showed every glorious curve, and her eyes shooting fire at him. He was getting uncomfortably hard watching her and imagining all that passion unfolding into other activities besides talking.

MacKenzie took a deep breath. "OK, fine. Here it is. I'm angry that you're so casual about sleeping around. I just can't hop from bed to bed, and it is driving me insane that you can. I'm jealous, Davey. Are you happy now?" She turned her head so he wouldn't see her eyes tear up. Damn him.

When Davey didn't say a word, MacKenzie looked up to see him smiling. Smiling! "What is so damn funny, Davey? You think it's funny to hurt me?" she asked in her low raspy voice.

The smile immediately left his face. "Jesus, no, MacKenzie! I would never hurt you. I'm smiling because you're jealous. Now you know how I feel every time another male is anywhere near you. You have nothing to be jealous about," he said, coming forward and putting his hands gently on her arms.

MacKenzie glared at him, backing out of his touch. "You went out last night, and it looked like you didn't get much sleep, so don't tell me I have nothing to be jealous about!"

"MacKenzie, I am going to be honest with you, always. I did have a date last night because I was angry that you said we weren't together, so I thought, what the hell, and called a woman. I showed up at her apartment and knew immediately that I had made a mistake. I told her something had come up and left and went to my brother's apartment and got shitface drunk so I could try not to think about you for just one fucking night. Even that didn't work.

"MacKenzie, why can't you just give in to this?" he asked urgently. "What we have is so good. The sex is off the charts, we work together like a dream, and we have so much in common. It's crazy not to give in to this and enjoy it."

MacKenzie just looked at him sadly. "Enjoy it for how long, Davey? A month, two months, a year? What is the shelf life for what you're asking? Can't you see, that I want more than that? I can't just live for the moment, knowing you are going to end it one day. I'm sorry, but I just can't. Why won't you just let a relationship develop and see where it takes us?" she asked imploringly.

Davey picked up the chair he was leaning on and set it down hard on the floor. "Stop it, MacKenzie! You're talking about marriage and children. That's not going to happen for me. Ever. Why won't you just stop being so fucking stubborn and let us enjoy ourselves without labeling everything!"

MacKenzie just saw red and marched up to him with her finger in his chest. "Fuck you, Davey!" she hissed and walked out the door. She had forgotten her bag, so she turned around as he passed her, walked out through the kitchen, and burst through the doors toward the bar. MacKenzie got her bag, wished Jack a happy birthday, and walked out of the restaurant. As soon as she was on the sidewalk, her phone rang. Tears were already falling as she took the call from Charlotte. "Hi, Charlotte. Is something wrong? Are you in labor?" she asked, sniffing.

Charlotte laughed until she heard MacKenzie sniffle. "Hey, what's wrong, sweetie?" she asked in her Irish brogue.

MacKenzie couldn't talk very well with the giant lump in her throat.

"Come to the apartment. The baby is fine. I'm alone, and I have to talk to you about something important. You can stay here tonight with me," Charlotte said.

MacKenzie really didn't want to be alone. "OK, I'm on my way," she said and hung up.

24

"Oh, darlin', I hate to see you hurting," Charlotte said after MacKenzie, in between crying spells, told her about the situation with her and Davey. "Do you think he will eventually change his mind?" she asked.

MacKenzie shook her head. "No, he's pretty final about not having a relationship or anything more. I guess the question for me is whether I agree to an affair and leave when he calls it quits or leave now before I'm completely crushed when he calls it quits."

Charlotte held up her finger. "There is one more option: I can go over there and hit him beside the head with a rolling pin!" she exclaimed.

MacKenzie laughed. It felt good to talk to Charlotte. They had spent many nights talking in their bunks in France. MacKenzie missed her. "Well, enough about me. You said you had something important to talk to me about," MacKenzie said, finishing her wine. They were stretched out on the giant sectional sofa in Charlotte's penthouse apartment.

Charlotte sat up, looking excited. "Oh, aye! I don't know if I ever told you, but every year, I apply to be a contestant on the reality show *Cupcake Battles*. The producer called me yesterday and said my shop was chosen along with three others from across the country," Charlotte said.

MacKenzie clapped her hands. "That's wonderful, Charlotte! Congratulations!"

Charlotte smiled wide and pointed to her big belly. "This is where you come in, love. I certainly can't compete in this condition, so I would like you to represent my shop for me. The publicity is out of this world, and they are handing out a large cash prize."

MacKenzie frowned. "How could I do that, Charlotte? I work long hours at the restaurant."

Charlotte nodded. "I know. I have thought of everything. The competitions are on Sunday, your day off. We would just have to get permission from Davey to have the film crew shoot where you work during the week. I know it's extra work for you, but the publicity for both my shop and Harmony will be huge. I will, of course, pay you for your work on Sunday, and I will let you keep the cash prize. Please say yes!" Charlotte pleaded.

"Charlotte, you know I would do anything for you, but I don't think Davey will ever agree to cameras in his restaurant. There's no way," MacKenzie said.

Charlotte nodded. "OK, fair enough. So are you saying that the only thing standing in your way is whether Davey agrees to the camera crew? Other than that, you're good to go?"

MacKenzie nodded enthusiastically. "Absolutely," she said, knowing Davey was never going to agree.

MacKenzie came downstairs Sunday morning to find Charlotte flitting around the kitchen making breakfast. Not just any breakfast but MacKenzie's favorite, French toast smothered in butter and syrup and a hot cup of coffee. Yum. MacKenzie looked suspiciously at Charlotte. "What's up?" she said with narrowed eyes.

Charlotte beamed. "Sit, sit. Dig in before it gets cold. I need you to have a full stomach when we discuss our schedules for *Cupcake Battles*." She took a big bite of French toast.

"Charlotte, I don't want you to get your hopes up..." MacKenzie began.

"He said yes," Charlotte interrupted.

MacKenzie stopped eating. "Excuse me?"

Charlotte nodded. "Davey said yes. I called him this morning, and we had a lovely chat. When he found out that you and I had bunked together and were friends, he said he would be glad to help out," she said, smiling.

"Wait, you already called Davey and told him everything? A camera crew is going to film *his* restaurant, and he was fine with that?" MacKenzie asked incredulously.

Charlotte laughed. "Aye! He said it would be great publicity for both our businesses, and he would be honored to help you, MacKenzie O'Riley," she said. "Oh, and I might have slipped and told him about the Baked Alaska incident." Charlotte was laughing harder now.

MacKenzie's face drained of color. "You didn't! How could you, Charlotte? I thought we were friends," MacKenzie lamented, not wanting to think about how she had set the kitchen on fire making that dessert. The school had had to relocate for a month while they gutted and rebuilt part of the kitchen. She would never live that down. Charlotte tried to stop laughing.

"Oh, MacKenzie, darlin', it was just an accident. It could have happened to anybody," she said in another fit of laughter.

Eventually, MacKenzie smiled. "You dirty rat! You wait until this baby is old enough to hear stories about its mother."

"You wouldn't," Charlotte said.

MacKenzie winked. "Maybe I would, and maybe I wouldn't," she said, feeling like she now had the upper hand.

Davey's phone rang as he waited on the sidewalk outside the Corner Market for MacKenzie. Garrett, the fifth Johnson boy, showed up on Davey's caller ID. Garrett owned and ran a hot new magazine based here in New York, *Metro Gent*. Davey knew that Garrett worked crazy hours, and he didn't get to see him as much as he'd have liked. "Hey, bro, what's up?" Davey said into the phone.

"Hi, Davey. All is well I hope?" Garrett asked.

Davey scowled. "I've been better," he said, looking at his watch. MacKenzie was late.

"Well, we will have to get together soon, but today I'm calling on business. My sources tell me that our Mac is going to represent Sweet Love in the newest season of *Cupcake Battles*. I've been meaning to do a story on her ever since she replaced Monsieur Lastat, so this will cover both stories in one. How would you feel about me sending over a reporter today to interview her and take some pictures of her in the restaurant?" Garrett asked.

Davey started pacing back and forth on the sidewalk. "Well, I don't see a problem, but there would be a couple of conditions. First, MacKenzie would have to agree to it. Second, send over a female reporter," Davey said, watching MacKenzie exit a yellow cab.

Garrett chuckled. MacKenzie walked over to Davey. "She is right here now, Garrett, why don't you ask her?" Davey said, handing the phone to MacKenzie, who looked confused. Davey listened as Garrett and MacKenzie talked, and she agreed to the interview later that day. When they hung up, MacKenzie handed the phone back to Davey and looked at him suspiciously.

"Why are you OK with all this? Charlotte said she talked with you about *Cupcake Battles*, and you were fine with that as well," MacKenzie asked as they walked into the market.

Davey took the canvas bag from MacKenzie's shoulder. "You've worked very hard to get where you are. You're very good at what you do, MacKenzie, and I think you should get recognized for it. You know not everything has to be a battle. I really do want you to be happy. Can we call a truce? I'm sorry about losing my cool at Jack's party. Friends?" he asked with sad puppy-dog eyes.

MacKenzie narrowed her eyes. "What kind of friends?" she asked in a low voice.

Davey's eyes sparkled. "At this point I guess I'll take any kind I can get, but you know what kind of friends I would like us to be, MacKenzie Rose," he said in her ear.

His husky voice and hot breath in her ear made her shiver. MacKenzie shook her head. "You're incorrigible," she muttered.

Davey smiled. "You have no idea."

The day was light and fun with Davey cooking and the whole crew dancing to sixties-era songs on the satellite radio. At least it was fun until one of the waitresses came into the kitchen to tell MacKenzie that some hot British guy was outside asking for her. MacKenzie walked out to the dining room with Davey right behind her to find a hot guy indeed.

The very handsome blond-haired, blue-eyed Brit held out his hand. "MacKenzie O'Riley?" he asked.

MacKenzie nodded.

"Hi, I'm Nigel Parker from *Metro Gent*. I believe my editor called you earlier about an interview?" he said.

MacKenzie smiled and shook his hand. "Oh, yes, Garrett called. Nice to meet you. You can call me Mac. Most people do. Would you like to get a booth?"

Davey injected himself into the conversation with "My brother sent you to cover the interview?"

Nigel looked uncomfortable and nodded. "Oh yes. I was actually across town when he called me and told me to come here, and I'm very glad he did," Nigel said, looking at MacKenzie.

Davey's jaw clenched. Motherfucker. Brothers were such pains in the ass. You just wait, Garrett, your day is coming, Davey thought as he watched Nigel walk with MacKenzie toward a back booth.

MacKenzie thoroughly enjoyed talking with Nigel. They talked of her schooling, her internship in Italy, her great affection for Maine, her love of books, and of course, her love of baking. After she told him she was an army brat, had lived all over the world, and in fact had lived for a short time in the English village that Nigel was from, they eventually made it back to the kitchen for some photos.

As Nigel was putting his camera away, he became nervous. "Mac, I was wondering if you were available on Saturday. We could do some sightseeing. You said you hadn't had a chance to see many touristy things, and neither have I. Maybe we could do that together?"

MacKenzie was just about to answer when Davey again injected himself into the conversation. "Um, I need your help on Saturday, MacKenzie, sorry," he said, wiping his hands.

Nigel smiled, clearly seeing what was going on, and nodded. "OK, maybe another time then. It was very nice to meet you, and this article should be in next month's issue. I'll make sure you get an advance copy," he said as he walked out the door.

MacKenzie turned to Davey with fire in her eyes. Davey just grabbed her hand, pulled her into his office, and closed the door. Immediately, his lips were on hers in a demanding kiss. He pushed her against the door so she could feel his body flush against hers. MacKenzie moaned and kissed him back just as demandingly. Their tongues danced and tasted each other until they were both gasping for breath. "Jesus, MacKenzie. You make me crazy. If anyone is going to show you this city, it's going to be me. Do you hear me?" he demanded.

MacKenzie smiled. "I'd like that," she said as she tilted her hips into him, and he moaned into her neck. "Now I have to get back to work. My boss will have my head if I don't get my work done," she said, wiggling out of his grasp.

Davey leaned his head on the door as she opened it. "It's not exactly your head I want right this minute, so you're right. You better run, little MacKenzie," he said, sounding pained.

Early Saturday morning, the knock sounded as MacKenzie was flying around her apartment putting snacks in her backpack. She ran to the door and threw it open to find Davey leaning casually against the doorframe. He looked delicious. His hair was a little mussed, and he hadn't shaved, which left a slight beard, very sexy. An old blue T-shirt with worn blue jeans and a brown leather belt. He wore sneakers from his family's company.

MacKenzie smiled brightly. "Hi. I'm just putting snacks in my backpack. I'll be ready in a few minutes. Come in," she said, walking back to the kitchen counter.

Davey looked confused. "Snacks?" he asked.

MacKenzie stopped what she was doing and looked up. "Ah, yeah. You'll thank me when you get hungry. I made some protein bars last night along with your favorite, peanut butter balls."

Davey smiled as he took in her attire. She had on skinny jeans with white Converse sneakers topped off with a New York Yankees T-shirt. Her hair was pulled into a ponytail, and her cheeks were flushed from rushing around. So beautiful and she had no idea.

Davey held up his hand. "OK, so hold on now, first things first. First of all, you look like a true tourist. Second, why snacks? We can just stop and eat when we're hungry. And third, most importantly, you have peanut butter balls here now?"

MacKenzie got out the container she was sending him home with and opened it. "I *am* a tourist, and so are you today. We are not going to have time to stop and eat. I have a full day planned, and yes, I have packed some peanut butter balls. These are for you to take home," she said as Davey dove into the container.

After he had eaten half the peanut butter balls, MacKenzie poured him a glass of milk to wash them down. Davey sighed. "The perfect breakfast. I'm ready for anything. Let's go!" he said, pulling her out the door.

MacKenzie laughed, slipped on her backpack, and tried to keep up. Once they got to the sidewalk, Davey turned to her. "OK, what's first on the tour?" he asked, opening the car door for her.

"MOMA, the Museum of Modern Art, of course," she said without hesitation.

Davey smiled. She was so friggin' adorable. "Of course. What was I thinking?" he asked flippantly.

MacKenzie got out her tour guide book, flipped to MOMA, and began to read the museum's history. "Did you know that the Museum of Modern Art was developed in 1929 by Abby Aldrich Rockefeller, the wife of John D. Rockefeller Jr., and two of her friends? They became known as 'the daring ladies.' Abby's husband was adamantly against the museum as well as modern art. He refused to give money for the venture, so they had to find funds elsewhere and had to move frequently. Eventually, John D. Rockefeller Jr. donated land for the current site and became one of its greatest benefactors," MacKenzie said, reading from her guidebook.

Davey laughed. "Hence, they stayed married. You women have all the power," he said, looking at MacKenzie.

MacKenzie rolled her eyes. "You're so full of it, Davey Johnson," she said as he parked the car.

Davey paid their way in, and they wandered through all the galleries slowly, contemplating each piece of art. Saving the best for last, MacKenzie was excited to see Picasso's *The Weeping Woman*. She stood and just stared at the painting. Davey came up behind her, drawing her close. MacKenzie smiled and leaned back on him. This felt so right, she thought. Davey dropped his head to her neck and gently kissed behind her ear. "Um, what do you think of this Picasso, Davey?" she asked distractedly.

Davey never looked up but continued to nuzzle. "Hmm, it speaks to me," he said into her neck.

MacKenzie laughed. "What is it saying to you?"

"It's telling me what a lucky guy I am to be spending the day with the most beautiful woman in all Manhattan," he whispered.

MacKenzie was finding it hard to breathe with his hot breath and lips on her neck. She turned and grabbed his hand. "You are a world-class flirt. Now stop trying to distract me. It's off to the Empire State Building now," she said, dragging a smiling Davey behind her.

At the Empire State Building, Davey navigated MacKenzie to the faster-moving line. She looked surprised. Davey leaned down and whispered in her ear. "I bought our tickets ahead of time. I kind of knew we would end up here eventually today."

MacKenzie's heart dropped. She loved him so much. "Thank you," she said in her husky voice. They stared at each other for a moment before the line moved to the elevators. MacKenzie cleared her throat. "Did you know that the Empire State Building was designed from the top down? The world's tallest building was completed on April eleventh,

1931, just four hundred ten days after construction commenced. The building coincided with the Great Depression, which left most of the offices unrented. New Yorkers mocked the building as the 'Empty State Building.' The building became profitable in 1950. More than thirty people have attempted suicide over the years. Only one person has jumped from the upper observatory. In 1932, Frederick Eckert ran past a guard and jumped a gate leading to an outdoor catwalk intended for dirigible passengers. Do you believe that? Dirigible passengers! How awesome is that?" MacKenzie asked the full elevator.

Davey pulled her close. "Perhaps now is not the time to tell us about those who have plummeted to their death from one hundred two stories," he whispered.

MacKenzie giggled and covered her mouth as the elevator doors opened. They walked out onto the observatory deck to a beautiful, clear, sunny day. MacKenzie got out her camera and snapped some pictures of the skyline and then of Davey, without him knowing. Both the view and Davey were breathtaking. As a fellow tourist walked by, MacKenzie asked him to snap a picture of her and Davey with the skyline in the distance. They posed, and the fellow took several photos before he told them to kiss. Davey took MacKenzie's face in his hands and kissed her tenderly. When he lifted his head, MacKenzie just stared at him until the man nudged her with the camera.

"Oh, thank you," she said and busied herself with putting her camera in her backpack. Sometimes her heart just felt overwhelmed with love, and it terrified her. How could she walk away from him? How could she stay, knowing that when it ended, she would be shattered, perhaps beyond repair? MacKenzie shook her head to push the thoughts away. Not today. Today was a rare gift, and she would enjoy every moment.

Davey took her hand, leading her back to the elevators. "Now I have a surprise," he said smiling.

"What? Oh, I love surprises! What is it?" she asked.

"Ah, just wait and see, grasshopper," he said with his forehead to hers. The elevator doors closed, bringing them to the sidewalk. As they started walking, MacKenzie stopped. "Is it a long walk? Should we eat something on the way?" she asked.

Davey smiled. "It's a few blocks, but yes, snacks would be great. It's past lunchtime," he said, looking at his watch.

MacKenzie dug out the protein bars and waters. They ate as they walked. "Mmm, these are really good, MacKenzie. Where did you get the recipe?" Davey asked, finishing his second bar.

"No recipe. I just threw ingredients together," she said.

Davey shook his head. "You're very talented. I'm glad I snagged you." He put his arm around her and pulled her close. They stopped in the theater district, directly in front of the theater where the musical *Wicked* was playing. The very one she had wanted to see since coming to New York!

Davey held up two front-row matinee tickets to *Wicked*. MacKenzie gasped. "No way! Davey, how did you manage front-row tickets?" she said incredulously.

Davey pretended to polish his nails on his chest. "I have my sources. Stick with me, kid, and you'll go places," he said in his best Cagney voice, and he ushered her into the theater.

The lights dimmed, and the magic began. MacKenzie was enthralled from the very first moment she saw Elphaba and Glinda. The play was based on the novel *Wicked: The Life and Times of the Wicked Witch of the West*, which she had read multiple times. The story never got old: two friends, Elphaba and Glinda, opposing personalities with the same love interest. Recipe for disaster if ever there was one and ultimately ending in Elphaba's fall from grace. Hence the title of Wicked Witch of the West. When the final curtain came down, MacKenzie felt like she had held her breath for the entire show. She had no idea that Davey had spent a good portion of the show watching MacKenzie's utter rapture at the performance. He had never met anyone who so openly enjoyed what life had to offer. She made life beautiful.

It was early evening when they exited the theater. MacKenzie's stomach growled loudly, making her giggle. "How about dinner at the best place in the city?" he asked, grasping her hand as they walked to the car.

MacKenzie looked suspiciously at him. "I thought we were taking a night off from Harmony," she said.

Davey nodded. "Well, the second-best place in the city," he said.

MacKenzie nodded. "OK, I'll bite. Where would that be?"

Davey looked offended. "My place of course. My apartment. How does angel hair pasta with shrimp and basil and a glass of red wine sound?"

MacKenzie groaned. "That sounds like heaven. Lead the way, my friend."

MacKenzie sat on a barstool watching Davey make dinner. He was so comfortable working around a kitchen. They had a glass of wine as Davey told her about some of the exploits he and his brothers had had. There was the bike jump they built that was so high that on the first attempt, Ty's bike went in one direction, and he went in another. One broken arm later, the same jump on the same day felled Davey with a broken foot. "My father was so mad at me because he had to go to the hospital twice in one day," Davey laughed.

"Oh my God! Why would you attempt the same jump after Ty got injured?" she asked laughing.

Davey smiled and pointed the paring knife at her. "That is exactly what my father asked, very loudly I might add. I guess I just thought Ty wussed out, and I could do better, and that is the exact reason why we visited the emergency room so much. We all think we can outdo one another," he said, smiling. "Thankfully, Jack never broke any bones because we were always very protective of her. Well, all of us except Caleb. Those two are like twins. They fought all the time and always tried to outdo each other. We all took Jack's being sent away hard, but Caleb... well, he took it especially hard. I'm so thankful she's back in our lives now." He leaned on the counter in front of MacKenzie. "I'm also very thankful that you are back in our lives, my sweet MacKenzie Rose," he said as he bent his head for a tender kiss. "Dinner is ready, my hungry lass," he said, nibbling on her lips.

MacKenzie moaned, forgetting about being hungry, and deepened the kiss. Davey moaned and stepped between her legs, spreading them apart. He wanted her so badly, but he also wanted her to eat because he knew she was hungry. Davey pulled away from the kiss and stepped back, taking her hands and leading her to the dining room table. He pulled out a chair, and she sat down. He walked back to the stove and prepared both their plates. MacKenzie smiled. Her heart was so full of love for this man. If only he could see that what they could have together didn't have to end.

Upon the first bite, MacKenzie was in food heaven. She couldn't stop moaning. "Davey, this is so good! The meal seems so simple, but the flavors are just bursting in my mouth." She took a sip of wine.

Davey smiled. "And that is the secret. You must keep it simple and let the spices work for you."

MacKenzie nodded. "KISS," she said.

Davey looked confused and leaned over and kissed her.

MacKenzie laughed and shook her head. "No, KISS means 'keep it simple, stupid.' That's what I repeat to myself when I start to stress over my baking. I've used that phrase since I was a teenager," she said.

"KISS," Davey repeated and nodded. "I like that."

Just then, his phone started ringing. Davey got up and walked to the bar to get it. "It's Marcus. Hey, bro, what's up? I'm just finishing dinner with the beautiful MacKenzie Rose O'Riley," he said, bending down and kissing her lightly. Mackenzie smiled.

Davey's face turned ashen, and he sat down hard. "When? Who found him?" he said brokenly. "Bear. Yeah, OK. I'll meet everyone there," he whispered. He dropped the phone and leaned over, his arms resting on his knees.

MacKenzie knew something bad had just happened. She knelt down in front of him with her hands on his knees. "Davey, what is it?" she asked softly. Davey just stared ahead, not moving. MacKenzie touched his face gently. "Davey, please, you're scaring me. Tell me what Marcus said," she pleaded.

Davey looked down at her and stared for a minute. "It's Dad. Marcus found him in his study. He'd had a heart attack. He's gone," he said in shock.

MacKenzie gasped, not able to breath. After several minutes she stood up and pulled Davey to the couch where she sat him down, straddled his legs, and hugged him tightly. Davey squeezed her tight, buried his face in her neck, and sobbed. MacKenzie stroked his head and held him for what seemed like hours.

Eventually, he pulled back. "I need to make some calls about work. I'm meeting Bear, Bobby, Ty, Teddy, and Garrett at the airport in the morning," he said.

MacKenzie took his face in her hands. "Davey, just call Mike and tell him what's happened. Between Mike, Luis, and me, we will be able to run the restaurant while you're gone. I will talk to Luis tomorrow. We've got this. Just go and be with your family. Don't worry about anything here, OK?"

Davey looked her in the eyes. "Do you have any idea how much that means to me? But with the competition coming up, you can't be tied to the restaurant every day," he said, pulling her hands away and kissing them.

MacKenzie shook her head. "Davey, you hire competent people, and you pay us well. Trust us to take care of things in your absence."

Davey teared up and nodded. "I will. Thank you," he whispered.

MacKenzie got up. "You call Mike, and I will clean up the kitchen," she said.

Davey stood up, grabbed her hand as she was walking away, and pulled her close. "Stay with me tonight. Please. I need you," he whispered into her hair. Tears fell from MacKenzie's eyes as she nodded and turned to the kitchen.

After she was done cleaning up, MacKenzie went to find Davey. She found him sitting hunched on his bed just staring at the floor with his phone in his hand. MacKenzie took the phone from his hand and laid it on the nightstand. She knelt before him and lifted his T-shirt over his head. Davey did the same with MacKenzie's T-shirt. Neither spoke as they both stood up and finished undressing. Davey shut the light off, and they crawled into bed. Davey pulled MacKenzie under him and began to slowly kiss her neck down to her breast and finally took her breast in his mouth and sucked gently. MacKenzie moaned and bowed her back off the bed. MacKenzie grasped his face and kissed him deeply, tasting him and nipping at his lips. Davey moaned.

MacKenzie pushed Davey onto his back and began kissing his neck. She slowly made her way across his broad chest and nuzzled her face in the soft hair on his chest as she made her way lower. Davey's manhood was standing proud as she embraced him and stroked him once. He gasped and lifted off the bed. "Oh Jesus, MacKenzie."

MacKenzie smiled and took him into her mouth. She loved the taste of him, and the moans of pleasure coming from him made her wet with need. MacKenzie stroked him, took all of him to the back of her throat, and groaned as she felt him grab her hair. He was in a frenzy as he bucked and moved her head to the rhythm he set. "MacKenzie, you need to stop. I can't hold back. Please. I'm going to come," he moaned as he tried to pull her up.

MacKenzie put her hand on his stomach to hold him back. She took him to the back of her throat again and again as she stroked him. Davey grabbed her hair and bucked and hollered her name as he came hard down her throat. She took all of him and kissed his thigh when he had stopped shaking.

Davey pulled her up into his arms. "Jesus, MacKenzie, I've never felt anything like that," he said softly.

MacKenzie snuggled in close and kissed his cheek. "Sleep, baby," she whispered.

Minutes later, Davey's even breathing told her he was asleep. MacKenzie lay there as her heart broke for the only man she had truly ever loved. She must have fallen asleep because the next thing she knew, she was having the most erotic dream she had ever had. It was dark, but she felt her legs being spread wide apart and then whisper-light kisses feathering over her core and the most delicious sensation of lapping and nipping before her clit was being gently suckled. MacKenzie woke up gasping for breath, not knowing where she was for a second until she realized she was with Davey, and it had not been a dream at all. Davey's large hand pushed her back on the bed as he continued his ministrations with his tongue. Good Lord, he was good at this!

MacKenzie moaned and writhed on the bed until she was so close to climaxing she cried out. "Davey! Please, I need you inside me!" Davey must have heard the urgency in her voice. He crawled up her body and in one swift stroke had buried himself inside her. They both moaned loudly with the complete ecstasy of being joined so fully. Davey began to move, and MacKenzie met him thrust for thrust. She felt the ball of tension deep in her belly, and it traveled throughout her limbs as she cried out Davey's name and fell over the edge. Davey gathered her close and put both hands under her buttocks to thrust deeper inside her. As he thrust faster and deeper, he too fell over the edge into the abyss. Completely spent, Davey and MacKenzie fell into a deep dreamless sleep.

25

MacKenzie woke to an empty bed and a silent apartment. She slowly got up and checked her phone. No messages. She made her way to the kitchen to find some coffee. Taped to the coffeepot was a note. "Thank you. I will call you when I can. Love, D."

What did that mean? Thank you for sleeping with me? Thank you for being there for me? Love? I love you? Love that you're part of my life? Love that you are a dear friend with benefits? Ugh, stop. Just stop. "It's a lovely note from someone I love dearly whose world just fell apart," MacKenzie said out loud to the empty apartment. She mentally shook herself. There was much work to be done.

MacKenzie called Mike and told him she would come to the restaurant after the competition later today. "MacKenzie, I think we are all set today, but if you would call when you're through to make sure, that would be great. If all is well, I will see you Monday morning," Mike said.

"Sounds good, Mike, bye," MacKenzie said, and she headed to the competition.

The competition was taking place at the International Culinary Center on Broadway. As MacKenzie walked into the vast kitchen, she saw four separate kitchen areas set up with cameras monitoring every move. A man with a headset came over to her. "O'Riley?" he asked.

MacKenzie nodded. "Yes," she said.

The man pointed to the last kitchen area. "You're in kitchen four. Go over and get ready to be interviewed before we start," he said, walking away.

MacKenzie looked over at kitchens one through three. Kitchen one had a stocky man about thirty with bleached-blond hair and a black goatee. Kitchen two had a man about twenty-five with long brown hair in a man bun and a beard. Kitchen three held a young woman with thick, wavy, dark-brown hair and big blue eyes. She had a beautiful hint of a Native American look about her. She looked like she was about to throw up.

MacKenzie walked to her kitchen area with a heavy heart. She felt so bad for the Johnsons. They had lost the patriarch of the family. It was a great loss, and the man she loved was in pain.

Mackenzie hung up her bag after she got out her music and set it on the counter. She watched as, one by one, the contestants were interviewed on camera. A British woman came into her kitchen area with a microphone. "Hi, MacKenzie, I'm Bridget. Tell us a little about yourself," she said.

MacKenzie smiled. "OK, well, as you said, I'm MacKenzie, and I currently live in New York City. I'm an army brat who has lived all over the world. I went to culinary school in France at Gastronomicom and interned at La Pergola in Italy. I currently work at a very upscale restaurant in New York City called Harmony, and I am representing the hottest cupcake shop in SoHo, Sweet Love, and I love to take long walks on the beach," MacKenzie said to laughter in the audience.

Bridget didn't look impressed. OK, then. Bridget went to stand before all four contestants.

"OK, here are the rules. You will have two hours to complete your cupcakes. You will use whatever ingredients you have in your kitchens. Each kitchen has different ingredients. If you have to use your computer at all, you will have ten points deducted. Your cupcakes will be graded on originality, presentation, and of course taste. Start the clock now." A buzzer went off, and everybody scrambled.

MacKenzie put her earbuds in. "Whoa, whoa, there. You can't listen to anything," Bridget said.

MacKenzie looked up. "What?" she asked.

Bridget walked over to her. "You can't listen to anything while you're baking," Bridget said.

"Says who?" MacKenzie said.

Bridget looked confused. "Um, I don't know. You just can't," she stammered.

MacKenzie plugged her earbud back in. "There was nothing in the paperwork you sent me that said I can't listen to music while I bake. It's how I work every day. If you have a problem with it, I can leave," she said, and she began going through her cupboards and fridge.

Bridget looked befuddled and walked away. MacKenzie made a quick inventory of her ingredients. Nothing special stood out, which disappointed her. She had just the basic flour and sugar ingredients, but she had some semisweet chocolate and some marshmallows. She sighed. OK, she would make a standby at the cupcake shop, moon rocks. They were a big hit at with the kids. She would put some buttercream frosting on them, and really, how could she go wrong? MacKenzie wondered if all the contestants got really bland ingredients. Moon rocks it was.

MacKenzie cranked her music and got to work. She finished before anybody else, so she made a nametag for her cupcakes and cleaned up her kitchen. When she was finished, she sat on her stool in the front of the judges. She brought out her phone and checked her e-mail. She had nothing from Davey or Mike at the restaurant, which was good news.

Eventually, the other contestants sat with her on the stools. Apparently, the other contestants had gotten the same bland ingredients because they had labeled their cupcakes chocolate with buttercream frosting.

It was all very dramatic as the judges made a big deal out of judging each cupcake. After the comments and tastings, the judges sat down and calculated each contestant's score. Out of a possible score of 10, the stocky blond from California, Steve, got an 8. The man bun and beard, Capone from Boston, got an 8.5. The beauty with big blue eyes, Riley from Alabama, got a 9. And last but not least, MacKenzie from New

York with the moon rocks got a 9.5. Everybody clapped in a truly disingenuous fashion.

MacKenzie had gone to collect her bag when she noticed the blue-eyed girl and walked over to her kitchen. She held out her hand. "Hi, I'm MacKenzie O'Riley. You can call me Mac. Congratulations, you did great today."

The girl shook MacKenzie's hand suspiciously. "How do you do? I'm Riley Garland. It's very nice to meet you, Mac," she said in a deep southern drawl. So proper.

MacKenzie smiled. "Where are you from again, Riley?"

Riley smiled. "Well, I'm from Alabama, ma'am," she said.

MacKenzie laughed. "Well, you can drop the ma'am and call me Mac. I have to make a call to my work, but if they don't need me, would you like to get some dinner with me, Riley Garland?" she asked.

Riley perked up. "Oh, yes, ma'am—oh, I mean Mac. I surely would love that!" she said, clasping her hands together.

"Great, let me just call the restaurant." MacKenzie dialed the phone. Mike picked up right away. "Hi, Mike, this is MacKenzie. Would you like me to come in to help close up tonight?" she asked.

"Hi, Mac, no, we're all set on this end. I will see you tomorrow after market as usual," Mike said.

MacKenzie smiled. "OK, I'll see you then." She hung up and turned to Riley. "It looks like you're stuck with me. I know the best place in the whole city to get a burger. Are you in?"

Riley genuinely smiled for the first time that day and nodded. "It would be an honor, Miss Mac," she gushed.

MacKenzie laughed out loud and linked arms with Riley. "Well, all right, then," she said as they marched out of the institute.

MacKenzie took Riley to her favorite diner. The two sat at the counter, catching Ed's attention at the grill. "Well, hey, there, sweet pea. Where have you been?" he asked.

MacKenzie smiled. "Hi, Ed. I've been working a lot, and I was recently asked to participate in a baking competition. Maybe you've heard of it—*Cupcake Battles*?"

Ed whistled. "You bet I've heard of it. The wife and I watch it all the time," he said.

"Well, this is Riley from Alabama, and she is also on the show." MacKenzie grinned and nudged Riley.

Ed leaned on the pass-through to the kitchen. "Well, I'll be damned. Good for you two! What can I make you two beauties tonight?"

"Well, I told Riley you make the best burgers in the city. We will have two, with fries and chocolate shakes, please," MacKenzie said.

Ed smiled. "Coming right up, sweet pea," he said.

"Tell me a little about yourself, Riley," MacKenzie asked.

Riley looked apprehensive.

"Well, how about I tell you about myself?" MacKenzie suggested.

Riley smiled. "I would really like that."

MacKenzie told Riley about growing up with the General and living all over the world. And how, as a result of moving so much, she had had very few friends, so she had started baking, and here she was baking for a living.

The food arrived, and as they ate, Riley felt a little more comfortable with MacKenzie and began to tell her story. "It sounds like you had a wonderful childhood. You're very lucky to have such great parents. I'm an only child, too. I don't know who my father is, and my mother...well, my mother has a hard time of it. She has a drinking problem and sleeps around a lot,"she said red with embarrassment.

MacKenzie touched Riley's shoulder for comfort.

"I know she loves me because she always protected me when the men she brought around started to come after me, but she can't take care of herself, let alone me. She's the only reason I stayed in Alabama once I grew up. I see now that I have to do what is right for me, and if I win this competition, then I will get job offers, and I can leave Alabama for good. I'll try to get her to come with me, but I know she won't."

MacKenzie continued to offer comfort as she squeezed Riley's shoulder.

"I was alone a lot as a child, so I began baking to pass the time. Eventually I baked and sold desserts to the local stores. A bakery in town hired me, and here I am. Oh, and on another positive note, I noticed you listen to music while you bake; I listen to baseball games when they're on. When I was little, we had a really old TV that only got one local station, which aired all the national baseball games. At first I just kept it on for the noise, but soon, I was totally involved in the games. Well, it's not a stretch to say I'm completely addicted to baseball, and I would give just about anything to watch the Boston Red Sox play in person."

MacKenzie shook her head. "Wow! You have overcome quite a lot to get here, Riley. You should be proud of yourself. Now tell me, what did you think of the burger and fries?"

Riley patted her stomach. "Oh my! That was the best burger I have ever eaten, and I hail from the South," Riley exclaimed, laughing.

"Riley, I noticed that you brought your suitcase with you. You must have just rolled into town. Where are you staying?" MacKenzie asked.

Riley turned red and looked away. "Well, I don't have much money, so I was going to try to find a shelter to stay in," she replied.

MacKenzie looked aghast. "What? No, please, you can stay with me at my apartment. It's really small, but it will be fine."

Riley shook her head. "No, I wouldn't feel right about that. You have been too kind to me," she said.

MacKenzie touched Riley's arm. "Please, Riley, I really could use the company right now," she said softly.

Something in MacKenzie's voice must have convinced Riley because she nodded her head with tears in her eyes. "OK, Mac, I would be honored to accept your gracious offer. Thank you."

When they finally arrived at MacKenzie's apartment, they were both exhausted. Riley loved the cozy little apartment. She ran her fingertips gently over the books in MacKenzie's huge bookcase.

"You like to read?" MacKenzie asked.

Riley smiled sadly. "Books were my only friends. My books have never let me down."

MacKenzie smiled. "See, I knew we were kindred spirits," she said brightly as she set up the cot beside the pullout couch that she slept on.

"Can I ask you a question, Riley? You don't have to answer it if you don't want to."

Riley smiled. "Ask me anything."

"Why didn't you have friends? I know why I didn't have friends; I was never in one place long enough to establish friendships. As sweet as you are, how come you don't have a boatload of girlfriends?" MacKenzie asked.

Riley sat cross-legged on the cot and smiled. "Well, you have to first understand that I come from a really small town in Alabama. We have a small main street and no stop lights. Everybody knows everybody else's business, so when your momma sleeps with just about every married man in town, well, you are not well liked. I was mostly just known as the town whore's daughter. I never had good clothes, and I smelled. I was the kid who was easy to pick on, so at a very young age, I just avoided everybody and escaped to my books and later baking," Riley replied matter-of-factly.

MacKenzie looked shocked. "Oh my God, Riley! I'm so sorry to have asked. That must have been awful," MacKenzie said as tears stung her eyes.

Riley looked shocked at MacKenzie's reaction. She laughed and went to hug MacKenzie. "Oh, Mac, please don't cry. I'm fine, really I know I'm not that smelly little girl anymore. I had a wonderful lady who loved me. I'm excited for my new life. Don't be sad for me. And besides, I do have a friend now."

"Yes, you certainly do, and so do I. But you probably should know that I am a big baby," MacKenzie said, laughing and sniffling.

Riley laughed with her. "OK, so noted," she said.

MacKenzie sent a quick text to Davey, telling him that her thoughts were with them all and good night. He responded quickly. "Good to be with siblings. Miss u. I will call you in the morning" his text read. MacKenzie smiled as both women settled down to sleep.

26

MacKenzie and Riley were making their way to Sweet Love when Davey called. "Hi, Davey, how are you?" MacKenzie asked.

"I'm doing OK. We're on our way to the funeral now. There are some things I need to talk to you about. Can I call you a little later?" he asked, sounding distracted.

"Of course. My parents will be there. Say hello to everyone for me, especially Jack," MacKenzie said, hanging up.

Riley touched MacKenzie's arm. "Is everything all right?" she asked.

MacKenzie shook her head. "Oh, some people who mean a great deal to me are going through a difficult time. I'll fill you in later tonight, maybe over a glass of wine."

They arrived at Sweet Love, and MacKenzie introduced the very-pregnant Charlotte to Riley. MacKenzie had asked Riley if she would be interested in working for Charlotte while she was in town for the competition. Riley was happy for the income. Charlotte was so thrilled to have Riley for the next three weeks.

MacKenzie gave Riley handwritten directions for the subway stops on the way to her apartment and a key. She was certain that Riley could handle everything. She took off to the market to start her week.

MacKenzie had just finished at the Corner Market with Jenny's help when Davey called. MacKenzie sat down on the bench in front of the market. "Hi, there. How was the service?" she asked.

"It was nice, and it was really good to see so many people turn out. I saw your parents there and Gracie. Listen, part of my father's will stipulated that all ten of us kids were to go to Harmony for three weeks. I guess to get us back to a place we once were as a family. I've got my laptop, so I can work and look over the invoices online, but I'm not going to be there for the day-to-day running of the restaurant. This is a lot to ask, but can I rely on you and Luis to take care of the kitchen end of things?" Davey asked.

"Davey, of course, don't worry about anything, really. I think it's great that your father is bringing you all together. You all need to grieve," MacKenzie said.

Davey sighed. "Yeah, I guess. It's just going to be so strange without him there at camp, you know? But enough about that. Tell me about the competition."

MacKenzie laughed. "Well, I made a new friend who I am also competing against, and she is staying at my apartment during the competition," she said smiling.

"What? Someone you don't even know is staying at your apartment? Come on, MacKenzie, that's not safe, and you know it!" Davey said, exasperated.

"It's fine, Davey, really. She's a lovely southern belle. But to answer your question about the competition, I scored the highest," MacKenzie said. "We have two other competitions, and whoever has the highest combined score wins."

"Wow, that's great. I'm not surprised that you scored the highest. You're still too trusting, though," he said in a low voice.

"I trust you, Davey," MacKenzie said softly.

"Yeah, and didn't I tell you you shouldn't? I mean it, MacKenzie, relationships aren't for me and never will be," he said firmly. "Listen, I gotta go, we're heading to camp now. I will be available by phone if you need me, and thanks again," he said and hung up.

MacKenzie sat stunned for a minute. Well, it looked like she had three weeks to decide if she was going to stay and be with Davey and be devastated when he ended it or leave when he came back with a broken heart but able to start again somewhere else. Why was this choice so hard to make?

27

Davey had forgotten how crazy it was with all his brothers and sister around. After the funeral, his sister, Jack, had had some sort of mental breakdown, and the whole house was in chaos. They had finally gotten her and Sam, her friend and counselor, off to the island for a couple of days of therapy when Davey decided he needed to go for a run.

As he went to his room to change, his eyes went directly to his bureau, to the envelope that Marcus had given him. It was from his dad. Davey was scared to death at what might be inside, which made no sense whatsoever, since he and his dad had had a great relationship. Later, he decided. He would open it later. He got his workout gear on and his music and headed out of the camp. Henry, Teddy, and Garrett were sitting at the bar.

"Off to the gym?" Henry asked sarcastically, knowing full well that the small town of Harmony, Maine, had no gym. Henry was the company attorney and had the driest sense of humor of the family.

"No, I'm going for a run. I'll be back later. I have to blow off some steam," Davey said, walking out of the house. He started running, and what kept circling through his head was his admonition to MacKenzie that "I don't do relationships, and marriage and kids aren't for me." He had felt like shit ever since their conversation. That was such an asshole thing to say to her. She was the absolute perfect woman, yet he wanted to use her and reduce her to a common mistress. He felt ashamed of himself because his father would be ashamed of him for his actions.

He ran faster, trying to outrun the shame, but he couldn't. He doubled over, gasping for air. What the fuck could he do? He had tried to stay away from her, but he couldn't. Seeing the General and MacKenzie's mom today was like a kick in the gut. Davey knew he was falling in love with MacKenzie. No, he *was* in love with MacKenzie, but he was still adamant that he wasn't interested in marriage. Why couldn't anybody see his point of view? What happened when it all went south? When the love of your life didn't love you anymore, or God forbid, they died? What happened then? You wanted to wither up and die for the rest of your life, that's what.

Well, no, thank you. He would happily just maintain the status quo of enjoying the moderately happy life he had built for himself instead of the spikes of high and pits of low that that kind of intense love brought. But all this still didn't help with MacKenzie. She deserved so much better than to be somebody's mistress. What happened if she found someone else? Davey's hands fisted just thinking about MacKenzie with another man.

Davey had made his way into town, so he decided to stop into the diner to see Gracie and grab some water. He sat down on the empty stool as Gracie made her way to the counter. "It was a nice service, Davey. Your Daddy will surely be missed around here," Gracie said, touching Davey's back and pouring him some water.

"Thanks, Gracie. I still can't believe he's gone," Davey said.

"He's with his Elsie now. He's a happy man," Gracie said, sitting down on the stool beside Davey.

Davey took a long drink of water. "Yeah, but Gracie, he was sad and alone half his life. What kind of life was that?" Davey asked.

Gracie smiled. "David told me you had a hard time with commitment. Do you know what he said to me? He said that even if he had known how everything was going to turn out, he wouldn't have changed a thing about his life. Elsie was the best part of him. He never, ever would have wanted to miss out on that no matter how much pain he endured through the years after she died. They had a love for the ages for sure. But your daddy believed that everybody had that kind of love come to them at least once in their lifetime, and it was up to them to grab it, or it would be gone forever. Your daddy wanted all you kids to experience the kind of love he and your momma shared," Gracie said, tearing up.

Then she nudged him with a sparkle in her eye. "Speaking of love, how is our sweet Mackenzie doing?"

Davey looked at Gracie with narrowed eyes. "MacKenzie is good, and why did you say, 'Speaking of love'?" Davey asked.

Gracie got up to wipe the counter. "Oh, no reason. Everyone loves MacKenzie. You know, when she first started coming in here, she was kind of an awkward teenager, but when she left for France, well, there wasn't a guy in this town who didn't wish for the attention of MacKenzie O'Riley," Gracie said.

Davey scowled.

"Just sayin'," Gracie said, holding up her hands. She got up and hugged Davey's back. "You'll do right by our MacKenzie. I know you will," she said, getting back to work.

Jesus. He felt worse than he had before. What the hell was he going to do about MacKenzie Rose O'Riley? He got up and ran for all he was worth back to the pond.

Davey ran up the stairs to the house to find Marcus, Henry, and Teddy playing guitar on the porch. Davey didn't stop but went straight to his room and closed the door. He grabbed the envelope from the top of the bureau and sat on his floor with his back to the bed. He slowly opened the envelope. An old picture fell out of the folded letter. Davey picked up the picture. He had never seen this photo. It was of his mom and dad in some sort of religious garden. They looked so young and happy. His dad was sitting on a stone bench beside a marble sculpture of Jesus with outstretched hands. His mother was sitting on his lap with her arms around his neck and the biggest smile on her face as she looked at the camera. His dad was looking at his mother with such love and devotion in his eyes. Davey stared at the photo for a while before he unfolded the letter and took a deep breath.

Hi there, son.

You're a good man, Davey, and I want to tell you how very proud I am of you. You have always been so smart and talented and such a go-getter. It doesn't surprise me at all that your restaurant is the finest in New York City. You have been the best son a father could ever ask for. Don't get me wrong, I didn't say perfect! I know the trouble you and your brothers would get yourselves into, and you and I made our fair share of emergency room visits. All those nights you thought I was asleep, and you and your brothers would sneak out of the house and go to those parties on the pond or at the pit. I knew when you left, and I also knew when you got home. You are all great kids. Your mom and I were very blessed to be part of your lives.

I know you think that I was always busy with the business, but it wasn't always that way. Your momma made sure there was plenty of family time. I remember the day every single one of you kids was born. You were born on a stormy winter day. When I say stormy, I mean a giant nor'easter that buried us in seventeen inches of snow. I remember looking out the window at the kitchen sink about early afternoon when your momma walked into the kitchen. She said I needed to put the plow on the truck, and I shook my head and said I would do it tomorrow when the snow stopped. She put her hand on my arm and said calmly. "No, you need to put the plow on now, please." I looked at her, and she smiled and patted her belly. "He's coming," she said.

Well, I never got used to hearing that, and I would fly around like a chicken with its head cut off. I got the plow on in record time, and it was the slowest trip to the hospital we ever took. I had to literally plow the road as we went along. We did that funny breathing all the way to the hospital, and your momma squeezed my hand with every contraction. For a tiny woman, she was strong! I thought she was going to break my hand before we reached the hospital! I pulled up to the entrance of the hospital and picked your momma up in my arms and ran into the hospital. She whispered in my ear. "David, just find a room fast, he's coming now. I have to push." As I ran into the emergency room, they recognized your momma and me, and they must have seen the terrified expression on my face because they just pointed to an empty room and scattered to find the doctor. I set your momma down on the bed and she started pushing and in about five minutes you were born into my big callused hands. A more perfect baby I have never seen. Your momma just laughed and said you were impatient "just like his daddy."

The doctor arrived and did what he needed to do, and we watched the rest of the storm from the hospital bed. I asked your momma what she would like to name you. She said if I didn't mind, she wanted to name you after me and your grandfather. She said she thought you were going to be the spitting image of the two Johnson men who came before you, and she was right. I know what you're thinking—sure, maybe in some things, but not everything. Well, let me tell you a story that may change your mind, son.

That picture with my letter was taken the day your momma agreed to be my wife. It was the happiest day of my entire life. You're probably rolling your eyes about now, thinking that that was fine for us, but it's not for you. Well, let me back up the story for you and tell you about the bump in the road. I met your momma at

Colby College. She was from the city on the West Coast and was the only child of very wealthy parents. Her parents wanted her to be a debutante, but she just wanted to have a simple life here in Maine doing something with music, like being a music teacher at a small school. It was the beginning of our senior year, and she said when she first saw me in the campus library, she turned to her friend and said she was going to marry me. We had never seen each other before that because we ran in completely different circles. I was the football quarterback and went to wild parties, and she was a member of the chess club and math club and probably many more clubs. She was always in the music department if she had any spare time.

That Friday night, she and her friend came to our big homecoming game. She stood right next to the field. I was just about to snap the ball to the receiver when I saw her. Well, she bewitched me the moment I laid eyes on her. I also got sacked good, too, for hesitating. I think I even suffered a concussion, for which I blamed her.

After that night there was never another woman for me. We were inseparable for the rest of the year. There was one thing that divided us, though. Your momma wanted to get married and have a houseful of children and lead a simple, quiet life. I, on the other hand, wanted to leave this hick state and move to New York and maybe pursue finance. Something fast paced, like Wall Street. I wanted to travel and live footloose and fancy-free, which definitely didn't involve a houseful of kids. Your momma and I saw eye to eye on just about everything, but on the subject of our future, we had an ocean between us. We solved this by simply not discussing the future. And that worked great until we were graduating and needed to start making plans for our future.

The day of our graduation, your momma came to my dorm room in the morning and brought me breakfast. I still remember, cinnamon buns and coffee. As we ate, she noticed an interview letter from a Wall Street banker on the nightstand. She picked it up and read it. I was scheduled for an interview the next week. I told her I was going to surprise her with it and that she could come with me and we would make it a vacation. I can still see the crestfallen expression on her face. She didn't mention it again, and the day was full of families and celebrating.

Toward evening I went to look for her, and her roommate told me she and her parents had left right after graduation. I thought that was odd, but I still thought she would call me to meet up in New York. When I got back to my dorm room to pack up, I found a letter from her telling me that although she loved me, she couldn't move to the city and live the life I wanted. She said she had decided to backpack around Europe for a little while before settling in Maine. She would leave me the itinerary for her journey and where she could be reached in Europe, in case I changed my mind about leaving Maine. She ended the letter by telling me she loved me and she was praying with all her heart that I would find her. Well, I was hurt that she left without telling me, but mostly I was angry that she expected me to change my dreams.

Well, I went to New York determined to get this job and make the life I thought I wanted. For days before my interview, I walked around the city with a hole in my soul bigger than the state of Maine. I was lost and lonely without Elsie. For hours I would sit and watch businessmen rush by all with stern, unhappy expressions on their faces. Where was everybody rushing to? I thought.

Well, I was offered that job, but I thanked them for their time and told them I wasn't able to accept their offer because my future was somewhere in Europe, and I needed to go find her. I didn't know what I was going to do for work, but I knew for certain that none of that mattered. The only thing that mattered was finding my heart and making my life with her. Everything else would work its way out one way or another, but I would be damned if some European bastard was going to steal my Elsie!

Well, I got on that plane and traipsed around Europe until I found her at the convent that Bebe lived in. I found her in that garden where the picture was taken, and I immediately got down on one knee and asked her to be my wife and move to Maine to build a life. She said yes and the rest is history, as they say.

You see, son, I do know how you feel about commitment and doing your own thing your own way, but when you fall in love with the other part of your soul, the only thing that matters is being together. Everything else is just details. You don't have a say in when you fall in love or who you fall in love with. When the love of your life shows up, it just happens. But you do have a choice after that about whether or not you're going to follow your heart. You can either grab that love and live within it or walk away from it so it doesn't ever have the power to destroy you. What you don't understand is if you choose to walk away from it, then you are already destroyed. Nothing else in your life will ever compare to how your feel when you're with your lover, best friend, the mother of your children and the very center of your universe.

Please don't walk away when it presents itself to you, Davey. I know you saw and felt my pain all those years like none of your other brothers or your sister did. Your momma was right—we do have a special bond. I want you to know that even if I had known that day in the office on Wall Street, as they were offering me the job of my dreams, that your momma would leave me way too soon, and I would have ten kids to raise, I still would have gone after her. She was the best part of me, and I have a little bit of her in each of you kids. She was the love of my life, and my only wish for you, Davey, is that you find that kind of love and hold onto it for as long as you can. I promise you it will be worth it.

With all my love,
Dad

Davey leaned his head back and just let the tears flow. God, he was going to miss his dad. He felt more conflicted than he ever had before. He took a little comfort that his dad knew what was going on in his life and had walked this very same road. His father was more observant than Davey had given him credit for. He still was no closer to sorting out his feelings for a certain beautiful flame-haired woman, but at least he had his brothers here to commiserate with. He jumped up and headed for the shower. He had better start dinner, or they all would starve.

28

MacKenzie leaned her head back against Davey's office chair and closed her eyes. She was so exhausted. She had been at the restaurant every day from the time it opened to closing, making sure everything ran smoothly. Between Mike, Luis, and herself, everything was fine, but she was tired. Thankfully, Riley had been busy at Sweet Love every day, so they both just fell into bed exhausted each night. MacKenzie liked having Riley there, and talking to her about Davey was helping. Each day, she felt closer to a decision regarding their relationship. Tomorrow was the second competition, and all she wanted to do was sleep. In fact, the very last thing she wanted to do was bake cupcakes.

Mike poked his head into the office. "We're all leaving. I'll lock the doors behind me," he said.

MacKenzie's eyes fluttered, and she nodded. She could hear a telephone ringing in the distance. She slowly came to with an awful pain in her neck from the odd angle her head had been resting at. She picked up the office phone. "Hello?" she said in a hoarse, sleepy voice.

"Jesus Christ, MacKenzie, why haven't you answered your cell phone? Are you all right?" Davey asked.

MacKenzie looked around for the clock, Midnight. Shit.

"What? Davey? Is something wrong? Why were you trying to reach me?" she asked.

"I just wanted to talk to you, and I got worried when you didn't answer your cell phone," he said in a softer tone.

"I guess I fell asleep. I was in your office going over the menus for next week when I just sat back and shut my eyes. I remember Mike coming in and telling me they were leaving and locking up, but then I must have fallen asleep," she replied, yawning.

"Baby, I'm sorry this is taking so much out of you. I feel helpless here. I promise I will make it up to you when I get home," he said.

MacKenzie laughed. "Oh, don't worry about it. We're fine, but I do miss you," she said quietly.

Davey's heart skipped a beat. "Oh, MacKenzie, you have no idea how much I miss you. Are you sitting at my desk?" he asked.

"Yes. Are you in bed?" she asked breathlessly.

"Yes. I wish you were right here with me. Do you want to know what I would do if you were here in bed with me?" Davey asked in a husky voice.

"Yes," MacKenzie whispered.

"I would start by kissing you and sucking on that sweet tongue of yours. Then I would travel down to your neck kissing and sucking and nibbling all the way. I would slowly unbutton your white shirt and move your white satin bra out of the way, and I would take your breast into my mouth and lick and suck." Davey heard MacKenzie's sharp intake of breath. "MacKenzie baby, I want you to touch yourself right now," he said urgently.

MacKenzie swallowed hard. "What?" she asked.

"You heard what I said, MacKenzie. I want you to unbutton your shirt and touch your breast and then I want you to unbutton your pants and put your hand on yourself inside your panties and touch yourself. Do it now," he said.

MacKenzie stood up. "I'm going to put the phone down for a minute," she said as she laid the phone down, unbuttoned her shirt and pants, and sat back down. "OK," she said.

Davey caught his breath. "OK, sweetheart, now I want you to spread your legs wide and stroke your lips gently. Don't go any deeper yet. And I want you to take your nipple between your fingers and squeeze," he commanded in a soft voice.

MacKenzie moaned, and she wanted to put her fingers deeper, but she didn't.

"Jesus," Davey said, hearing her moan.

"Davey, I need more," MacKenzie whispered, arching her back.

"I know, sweetheart, not yet. Now I want you to slowly worry your nipple between your fingers, squeezing every so often. I want you to put two fingers inside your pussy and move them gently back and forth, careful not to touch your clit."

MacKenzie gasped and moaned. "Davey," she said on a moan.

"Yes, baby? Tell me what you need," he said huskily.

"You. I need you inside me. I want you naked, Davey, and I want you to stroke yourself very slowly with a tight fist. Just like you were entering me, oh, so slowly," she said in her raspy voice.

Davey caught his breath again and moaned as he gripped himself and did as she said. "Jesus, MacKenzie, don't stop. Put your fingers inside yourself and pull out like I was pumping into you. I need to go faster, babe, tell me to go faster," he said as if in pain.

MacKenzie took her fingers deep and moaned.

"MacKenzie, Jesus, tell me, I'm dying here," he said urgently.

"Oh, Davey, faster, pump yourself faster, tighter, harder! I'm going to come, Davey! Oh my God!" MacKenzie hollered and moaned.

"Fuck! Jesus, baby, I'm right there with you! When you pull your hand out, touch your clit with the top of your hand hard as you shove right back inside your pussy. Hard and fast, baby!" he said, and MacKenzie did as he said. She moaned and came apart in a much-needed orgasm.

Davey heard her loud moan and stroked himself fast and hard before coming long and hard into his hand. The line was silent for a minute before MacKenzie gulped some air. "Oh my!" she said.

Davey laughed as he leaned down to grab his T-shirt off the floor to clean himself up. "MacKenzie, fuck, that was amazing. Now I want you to—no, scratch that, I'm going to call a cab for you right now to take you home. I want you to text me that you got home safe. Get some sleep and good luck at the competition tomorrow," he said.

"Oh, thank you. Good night, Davey," MacKenzie said softly.

"Good night, sweetheart," Davey said, hanging up.

Sweet mother of God! She had never done anything like that before. Smiling, MacKenzie walked out front to wait for the cab.

29

MacKenzie and Riley showed up at the competition arm in arm, laughing at Riley trying to sound British with her Southern accent. The two unfriendly male contestants were already at their kitchens and glared at them as they strolled in. MacKenzie and Riley air-kissed, wished each other luck, and headed to their kitchens. They weren't allowed to look in the cupboards or fridge at what they had for ingredients until the buzzer went off, signaling the start of day two of the competition.

MacKenzie put her apron on as the host came around and interviewed each contestant. MacKenzie had her usual baking uniform on, but she was wearing a yellow scarf with little red flowers as a headband, which added some color to her outfit. After the interviews were complete, the buzzer went off, and MacKenzie opened her cupboards and fridge. She was immediately disappointed to see just basic ingredients. There was, however, a ton of chocolate and some buttermilk, so she decided on her old standby, chocolate cupcakes with fudge ganache. She felt it was a little too basic, but with the ingredients she had to work with, this was the best she could come up with. She had made so many of these at Sweet Love that she could make them blindfolded. They were the number-one selling cupcake at Sweet Love. The masses couldn't be wrong. She plugged in her music and began baking. Again, MacKenzie was done before everyone else and sat on the stool, checking her e-mail on her phone.

When the others were done, they joined her to wait for the judging. Riley sat next to MacKenzie, looking like she was going to throw up. MacKenzie patted her back. "Relax, Riley. You've got this, girl," she said, smiling.

The judges came out and went through the long and painful process of tasting the cupcakes and critiquing each contestant. When the scores were processed, all four contestants received an 8, which put MacKenzie in the lead by just half a point and Riley in second place.

Interesting predicament, thought MacKenzie. MacKenzie had decided that she wanted Riley to win this competition, but she wasn't sure how to go about making that happen. She couldn't let her win. MacKenzie wouldn't want to win that way, and neither would Riley. Riley *needed* to win, whereas MacKenzie had a great job and didn't really care one way or another. She had acquired a new friend, which was worth way more to MacKenzie than the title of champion cupcake maker.

When they had grabbed their stuff, MacKenzie linked arms with Riley. "I think we need to go out to celebrate, and I know just the place," MacKenzie said as they hit the sidewalk.

Riley laughed. "I agree! I got paid today, so the first round is on me."

MacKenzie hailed a cab, and they went to the Upper East Side to a bar that she had wanted to visit. Texas Hold'em was a country bar that had a mechanical bull. One day when she passed the bar, she knew she needed to go there with Jack.

When they climbed out of the cab, Riley looked up to see the blinking neon bull, and she clapped her hands. "Now we're talking, MacKenzie Rose," Riley said as they entered the bar.

When they walked in, there were groups of people line dancing. MacKenzie looked nervous. "I don't know how to line dance. Do you?" she asked.

Riley looked offended. "Are you kidding? They teach that in kindergarten in the South, sugar. Don't worry about anything. I will have you line dancing like a cowgirl before the night's out!" she exclaimed as they walked into the bar.

Immediately after they sat down, two shots of Patron were set in front of them. They looked at the bartender, confused. He motioned to two cowboys at the other end of the bar. The ladies clinked glasses, saluted the gentlemen, and downed the shots. Then they ordered vodka and cranberry. When they had their drinks, Riley grabbed MacKenzie's hand. "Take your drink, and I'll give you a lesson. Just watch my feet and do the same thing," she said.

MacKenzie had never laughed so hard at herself. She was always going right when she should be going left and vice versa. They finished their drinks, and MacKenzie motioned toward the mechanical bull. Riley laughed and shook her head. "I don't think that's a good idea, Mac. Have you ever done that before?" she asked.

MacKenzie laughed. "Um, no I haven't had the pleasure yet," she said, signing the disclosure agreement. Just then, her phone rang. "Hello?" she hollered over the music.

"MacKenzie, where are you? I can barely hear you over the music!" Davey shouted.

"Oh, hi, Davey! Here, talk to Riley for a minute," she said and handed the phone to Riley while a big handsome cowboy helped her onto the bull.

"Hi, this is Riley. Is this Davey?" Riley asked.

"Um, hi, Riley. Yes, this is Dave. What's going on? Where are you?" he asked.

Riley laughed. "Oh, we're at a bar called Texas Hold'em, and MacKenzie is being helped onto a mechanical bull by a big handsome cowboy. Oh no, bull's moving now! She's doing so good for a beginner. Oh, it's going faster now! Oops, it just threw her onto the mat. Oh, there's that cowboy again," Riley said, giving a play-by-play.

"Jesus Christ, is she OK, Riley?" Davey hollered.

"What? Oh, yeah, she's fine. Here she is. I need to beat her time. Bye! Nice talking to you!" She handed the phone to MacKenzie.

"Davey?" MacKenzie asked.

"Yes, it's me! Who did you expect to be on the line? What the hell is going on, MacKenzie?" Davey asked, frustrated.

MacKenzie laughed. "Oh, I'm sorry, honey, this is so much fun. We had a stressful day baking. We all tied today, which makes me only a half a point ahead of everybody else. Riley and I came out to celebrate, but don't worry, I called Mike to make sure everything was OK at the restaurant before we came to the bar," she said.

"I don't care about that, MacKenzie. You deserve a break, but I don't like you at a bar alone," Davey said.

"But I'm not alone. Riley is with me," she said as the waitress brought over two more shots of Patron. "Wait, we didn't order these," MacKenzie said to the waitress. The waitress nodded to the bar. "Oh, all righty then," MacKenzie said.

"Who the fuck is sending you drinks, MacKenzie?" Davey growled.

MacKenzie laughed as she downed the shot. "Oh, Riley is on the bull. It's started. God, she is good at this. Oh my God, it's going so fast, and she is staying on! Oh no, it just threw her a long ways! There's that nice cowboy helping her, though," MacKenzie said. "Oh, sweetie, enough about me. How are you doing?"

Davey sighed. She was too sweet for her own good. "I'm doing OK. It's good to reconnect with my brothers and Jack," he said wearily.

"I miss you," MacKenzie said in her raspy tone.

"I know. I miss you, too, baby. One more week, and I will be home," he said.

"I'm glad," MacKenzie said honestly.

"MacKenzie, I don't like you being at a bar."

MacKenzie smiled sadly. "Well, you don't really have that say, do you, Davey?" she asked with tears in her eyes. There was a long pause.

"No, I guess I don't, but I still don't have to like it," he said.

MacKenzie smiled. "Well, if it's any consolation to you, I'm glad you don't like it. Oh, Davey, I've got to go. They want me to ride the bull again. I'll talk you to you tomorrow at work, honey. Bye." MacKenzie handed the phone to Riley and took the cowboy's hand so he could lead her to the bull.

30

MacKenzie couldn't quite pinpoint where the pain was the greatest: her head or every single other part of her body. She lay there, mentally trying to prepare herself for the huge effort of crawling out of bed. MacKenzie heard Riley moan. She started laughing, and pretty soon Riley was laughing hysterically with her.

"What was I thinking?" MacKenzie asked, still giggling.

"I think even my eyeballs hurt," Riley said painfully, which started the laughter again.

MacKenzie slowly crawled off the bed and made her way to the coffeepot. "Maybe a shower will help," she said, walking to the bathroom.

"One can only hope," Riley said, still lying on the cot not moving. The shower did help a little bit, along with a couple of pain relievers and coffee. MacKenzie walked Riley to the subway before hailing a cab to take her to the market.

Jenny helped MacKenzie shop, and even Jenny could see MacKenzie wasn't herself. She was hungover for sure, but something in MacKenzie's spirit was off. She knew what it was, but perhaps if she just didn't think about it, it would magically go away, and Davey would let go of his fear of commitment. MacKenzie rolled her eyes. Yeah, that wasn't going to happen in her lifetime. Maybe she should just go back to Maine for a while to figure things out. She could help Gracie at the diner and see her mom and dad.

No! She was not going to crawl back home and disappear. She had to make a life for herself that ultimately didn't include Davey. That could be sooner or later, but she only had a week to decide.

By the time MacKenzie had made it to the restaurant, her arms felt like they were going to drop off. Mike was in the kitchen when MacKenzie heaved the bags on the counter. "Wow, those are heavy," she sighed.

Mike laughed. "I bet you wish Dave was here to help you."

MacKenzie nodded. "You can say that again! I hope Luis didn't need anything. Davey shops on Mondays, too," she said, putting her supplies away.

Mike leaned on her counter. "Dave doesn't shop for the restaurant on Mondays. Tell me, didn't you ever wonder why Dave met you at the market on Monday mornings? It wasn't because he needed to shop, MacKenzie. He has people to do that. He met you on Monday mornings because he wanted to see you and help you with the bags. And furthermore, before you came to work here, Dave never even came in on Mondays until evening."

MacKenzie stopped and stared at Mike. She shook her head. "Mike, I know you're not stupid. You can see there is something between Davey and me, and it's not complicated, but sometimes the simplest situations are the hardest to deal with. I love Davey, and I have since I was seventeen years old. I know Davey has feelings for me, but he is totally against commitment, and I can't just be another of his temporary partners."

Mike nodded. "I understand. What are you going to do?" he asked quietly.

MacKenzie shrugged. "That's the million-dollar question. I have no idea, but I need to decide before he gets back because I can't think when he's around me."

Mike came around and gave MacKenzie a hug. "Thank you for telling me. I'm here if you need anything," he said, squeezing her.

MacKenzie yelped, and Mike took a step back. "What's wrong?" he asked.

MacKenzie rubbed her arms. "Um, it could have something to do with bull riding," she said.

Mike rolled his eyes. "Is that what they're calling it these days?" he asked, walking out of the kitchen.

MacKenzie gasped. "I was riding a bull! It was real! I mean, a real mechanical bull!" she hollered after him.

The day was brutal, but at the end of the evening, she poked her head into Davey's office where Mike was going over the day's receipts. "Did Davey call today?" MacKenzie asked, concerned.

Mike looked up. "Oh, yeah, he called this morning when you were at the market," he said.

That kind of hurt. He must be mad at me for going out to the bar, she thought. "Oh, good. I was just wondering," she said with a small smile.

Mike grinned. "If it makes you feel any better, he told me to take it easy on you today because you were probably tired from the competition."

MacKenzie's eyes teared up. God, she loved him. He was so sweet and thoughtful. She waved to Mike and walked outside. She was going to walk tonight. She pulled out her phone and dialed Davey.

"Hello," a woman's voice said. MacKenzie was stunned silent. "Hello?" the woman said again, less patient. It wasn't Jack.

"Um, hello. Is Davey there?" MacKenzie asked.

"No, they all went up to the house for more beer. Any message?" she asked.

"Who is this?" Mackenzie asked.

"Stephanie."

MacKenzie's heart sank. "Ah, no, no message," she said and hung up. This is what she was going to have to get used to when Davey decided to end things between them. It would kill her, she thought as tears began to fall.

On Wednesday afternoon, Mike came into the kitchen looking for MacKenzie. He popped his head into the break room where she was just finishing her lunch. "Someone named Nigel is asking for you," Mike said.

Nigel from the magazine.

MacKenzie jumped up and went to the dining room where the handsome Brit stood. MacKenzie smiled. "Hi Nigel, it's nice to see you. Do you have time for some tea?" she asked.

Nigel smiled brightly. "That would be lovely," he said.

"Great. If you go to the same back booth we had before, I will bring us some. Would you like a piece of coconut cake I made?" she asked.

Nigel rolled his eyes back. "Would I ever!" he said, walking to the booth.

MacKenzie took off her apron, gathered the tea and cake, and made her way to the booth.

"I came by to give you an early copy of the magazine. It hits the stands tomorrow morning," Nigel said, handing her a copy of the *Metro Gent* with a picture of her on the cover, leaning on her counter with her arms crossed. She had her chef's white jacket on and her black slacks. Her hair was pulled back like she wore it every day at work. She was smiling, and she distinctly remembered Nigel making some comment about not looking so bloody angry and smiling at the time the picture was taken. The headline caught MacKenzie's attention and made her blush.

"New York's Sweetest Cupcake."

MacKenzie flipped to the article, which was mostly just factual information about her life and schooling. The article gave a plug to Davey's restaurant and Sweet Love, and mentioned her appearance on *Cupcake Battles*. There was a blurb at the end, indicating that if you wanted the best dessert in New York, you could find it at Harmony made with love by a beautiful and single flame-haired pastry chef named Mac. Mac looked up to find Nigel looking at her.

"Sorry if that last part makes you uncomfortable, but it's all true," he said, shrugging.

MacKenzie smiled. "Well, I appreciate that," she said.

They finished their cake and tea, and MacKenzie told Nigel that she had to get back to work. As they walked to the entrance Nigel hesitated. "Would you like to have dinner with me sometime?" he asked.

MacKenzie was a little surprised. "Oh, yes, that would be nice, but it will have to be later because I'm working every day but Sundays, and that's only because of the competition."

Nigel nodded. "OK, I'll take it. It's not a no. Good luck on the competition," he said, kissing her cheek and leaving.

31

"'Beautiful and *single* flame-haired pastry chef'? What the fuck, Garrett?" Davey said, reading the excerpt out loud. All ten siblings and Jared had been sitting on the porch when FedEx dropped off the magazine to Garrett.

Garrett shrugged. "The information is all true, and you, my brother, have the power to change her status to 'hands the fuck off, she's taken,'" Garrett retorted.

Davey threw the magazine down on the piano. "Oh, that's rich, Garrett, coming from one of New York's most eligible bachelors listed in *Forbes*. And besides she *is* taken, kinda," he said with less heat.

"Kinda?" Henry asked. "What does that mean?"

Davey looked uncomfortable. "Well, she is kinda deciding about us," he said, looking out the window.

Bobby sat forward. "No fucking way! Are you...? You're not asking her for one of your no-strings-attached little flings, are you? Because I think the General literally has people to take you out if you hurt his daughter, unless he takes you out himself, of course," he said.

Bear spoke up. "Well, not if we kick your ass ourselves first."

"She deserves better than that, Davey," Ty said quietly.

Davey got up and started to pace. "I fucking know all this! I never want to hurt MacKenzie."

Jack went over to Davey and laid her head on his shoulder. "I trust you to make the right decision, Davey. We love you both, but just know that if you hurt my best friend, well, what I did to Caleb is nothing compared to the hell I will unleash on you," she said, smiling as she walked out the door toward the pond.

"Fuck me," Davey muttered. He looked at Marcus as Marcus placed a finger to his nose and declared with a smile, "Yup, I'd say you are well and truly fucked, little brother."

The night seemed endless as Davey tossed and turned fitfully. The dream was so vivid and real. It was raining, and he was standing on a hillside looking at a graveyard service. It was cold and raw. He could tell it was Maine by the huge pine trees along the edge of the cemetery. There were lots of people there, and he started to recognize faces. There was Gracie, the General, and MacKenzie's mom. Standing beside MacKenzie's mom was that British reporter who interviewed MacKenzie, and he was holding the hands of a little red-haired boy and girl. The children were crying. Davey looked around for MacKenzie, but he couldn't see her. Suddenly, hands on his back started to rub reassuringly. Davey looked to his right and saw his mother smiling at him, and then to his left, he saw his father, who was also smiling.

"Hello, son," his father said and patted his back. His father looked happier than Davey had ever seen him. He was beaming and so young.

His mother touched his arm. "Davey, we're so proud of you, son. Don't be sad because we will take good care of her." His mother looked exactly the same as he remembered her. Beautiful, smiling blue eyes, and long blond curls piled on her head. She, too, looked so happy.

Davey was befuddled. "Who will you take care of, Momma?" Davey asked.

His mother pointed to the casket. "Why, MacKenzie, of course," she said.

Davey's heart stopped beating. "What do you mean?" he whispered.

David cleared his throat. "Son, MacKenzie moved on and got married after you ended it with her. She married and had a family. One evening, she and her husband were fighting, so she decided to take a drive to clear her head, and a moose ran out into the road. She couldn't stop in time and was killed. She never stopped loving you, son," his father said.

Davey shook his head violently and ran to the casket. "No! That's not true! She is in New York taking care of the restaurant for me! I won't let her go! She is not going to marry that fucking Brit! I won't let her!" he screamed, but no one seemed to be able to hear him but his parents.

His mother walked to him. "Sweetheart, you made your choice. You chose to walk away from love. You were too afraid to open your heart. You never stopped loving MacKenzie and always regretted your decision. But don't worry, son, we'll look after her." His mother took his father's hand and starting to walk away.

"No, wait! What if I don't walk away? Will she still die?" Davey hollered after them.

Elsie looked over her shoulder. "Sweetheart, being afraid to love is not living. No one knows when it's their appointed time. That's why it's so important to not be afraid and to live life to its fullest. Love is the greatest gift we can give each other, Davey. Don't waste your gifts," his mother ended as she and his father faded away.

Davey sat bolt upright in bed and gasped for air. Big deep breaths of air. He swung his legs over the side of the bed, grabbed his phone with shaking hands, and dialed MacKenzie's number. After several long rings, she finally picked up.

"Hello," she said in the sleepy, raspy voice he loved.

"MacKenzie, hi, sweetheart," he said softly.

"Davey? Is something wrong?" she asked, not quite awake.

He laughed. "No, sweetheart, everything is finally right. I just needed to hear your voice. Go back to sleep. I love you, MacKenzie," he said.

"Mmm, I love you, too, Davey. Night." The phone went dead.

Davey just stared into the darkness, waiting for his heartbeat to return to normal. When he got home, he would beg her to forgive him for being such an ass. Davey beamed, feeling like the weight of the world had been lifted off his shoulders. He got up and dressed in the dark in a pair of shorts and a T-shirt, found his running shoes, and headed to the pond to watch the sun rise. He had a lot of planning to do, he thought as he started jogging to the beach.

32

"Hello?" MacKenzie fairly shouted into the phone for the fourth time before sighing and hanging up. The magazine had hit the stands today, and all sorts of weird stuff was happening. Three times, the hostess had come in that afternoon to tell her she had a phone call, and each time she could hear someone breathing, but they wouldn't speak, so she just hung up. That evening, Mike had come into the kitchen to ask her to come out into the dining room because customers had read about her and wanted to tell her how much they had enjoyed their dessert. It was always a pleasure to talk to happy customers, but it was starting to interfere with her work.

On Friday and Saturday, Gabe, the cook's assistant, had called out sick, so they were very shorthanded. MacKenzie went back and forth between her job and helping Luis. She was expecting Davey to arrive sometime Saturday, but she didn't know exactly what time. He had called and left her a message saying something had come up with Jack, and he would be later than he thought. By the time the evening rush was over, MacKenzie could barely stand. Mike ordered her to go home to rest for the last competition on Sunday.

As MacKenzie was climbing the stairs to her apartment building, her phone rang. "Hello," she said tiredly.

"Hi, sweetheart, I'm home. I just got to the restaurant. I'm sorry I missed you," Davey said.

"Oh, Davey, I'm glad you're home. Is everything all right with Jack?" she asked.

"Yes, she'll be OK. I'll fill you in when I see you. Can I see you tomorrow after the competition? There are some things I want to talk to you about," he said softly.

"Um, yeah, sure. I'll call you when I'm done. I have some things I want to talk to you about as well."

"I missed you so much, MacKenzie," Davey said.

MacKenzie smiled. "Me too," she said.

"OK, well, I'll let you rest. Good luck tomorrow, sweetheart."

"Good night, Davey," she replied and hung up.

— ⌣ —

The last competition was a little different from the others as the contestants were able to write out what they needed for ingredients and make whatever kind of cupcake they wanted. There was only one thing that MacKenzie could do that might help Riley win the competition. MacKenzie had decided to make a variation of a croquembouche, a French dessert of *choux* pastry balls piled into a cone and bound with threads of caramel. But instead of the multiple pastry balls in a cone, she would make one large ball, a cupcake-size ball. In Italy and France, a full-size croquembouche is often served at weddings. She was counting on the French pastry chef on the judging team to have an issue with this as a cupcake. It could backfire on her, and it could be seen as innovative and cutting edge. But knowing the French, MacKenzie was counting on the judge to make a stink. That way, MacKenzie could just shrug and say, "Oh well," and Riley would be the winner, fair and square.

Riley and MacKenzie got situated in their kitchens, making sure all the ingredients they had requested had actually been purchased. Laying on the counter was a single red rose. MacKenzie looked around and didn't see anybody she knew or a note anywhere. She found a glass to put the rose in and set it on her counter. There seemed to be more people around during this competition than the previous ones. It wasn't publicized where and when the competition was being held, but it wasn't a secret either. Once the lights were turned on, it was impossible to see out into the crowd. Everyone was told to take their places, and the buzzer sounded for the baking to begin. MacKenzie put her earbuds in and was soon lost in the music and baking.

The bell signifying the end of the competition sounded, and the contestants took their stools in front of the judging table. The crowd and lights were to their backs. Davey stood in the back watching MacKenzie's familiar mannerisms as she baked. He smiled, watching her perfect ass bounce to the beat of the music. God, he loved her. Two men appeared beside Davey speaking rapid Italian. What immediately got Davey's attention was the mention of MacKenzie's name. Davey looked over at the men. The man who seemed most agitated was smaller than Davey. The other man was a giant with crossed arms, looking all around. When the giant spotted MacKenzie, he tapped the smaller man and pointed. "Ah, there is *mio amore*," the smaller man said.

Davey's fists clenched. He didn't know much Italian, but he knew *amore* meant love. Davey crossed his arms. "Do you know MacKenzie?" he asked the smaller man.

The man looked surprised and smiled and nodded. "Oh yes, I know her very well, indeed. I am hoping to make her my bride soon," he replied.

Davey's heart dropped. Roberto. Davey had never, ever wanted to punch somebody as much as he wanted to punch this gigolo who had hurt his MacKenzie. "You must be Roberto," Davey said.

"Yes, that would be me, and who might you be?" Roberto asked, also garnering the attention of the giant.

"I'm Dave Johnson. MacKenzie and I work together," Davey said.

"Oh yes, MacKenzie has told me all about your restaurant. Well, I'm sorry to have to report to you that MacKenzie will not be in your employ much longer, Mr. Johnson. Along with trying to win back my lovely MacKenzie, I am here to offer her the head pastry chef position at La Pergola. The most coveted position in pastry realms worldwide," Roberto announced smugly.

Davey felt like he was going to be sick. The bell sounded for the end of the competition, and the contestants sat before the judging table. The judges were looking over the cupcakes when the French judge began speaking loudly to the other judges. Davey looked at the table and immediately knew what MacKenzie had done. Jesus. MacKenzie had known this woman Riley for three weeks and had decided that Riley needed to win more than she did. MacKenzie was too trusting for her own good.

The judges sat down and addressed the contestants while the cameras kept rolling. The French chef, in very broken English, admonished MacKenzie for making what she called a croquembouche cupcake when in fact it was simply a profiterole or cream puff topped with spun caramel sugar. For that faux pas, she was disqualified for this round, which would give her the lowest score.

All at once a loud yell to the right of the kitchen commanded everyone's attention. "No! You can't do that! She deserves to win, and I won't let you take that away from her!" the voice yelled.

Around the corner, a large, stout man with gray hair and the start of a scraggly salt-and-pepper beard came into view, waving a gun. People screamed and tried to back up before he hollered for everyone to stay still. Davey was frozen in place watching MacKenzie. The man pointed the gun at the French judge. "Take back what you just said. Sara is the winner of this battle. Say it!" he hollered, waving the gun.

The French judge nodded vigorously. "Yes, yes of course. Miss O'Riley is the winner of the *Cupcake Battles*, monsieur," he said shakily.

The gunman was getting more agitated by the minute. "Her name is Sara Jones, and she is my fiancée," he said, facing MacKenzie and holding out his hand.

MacKenzie flinched. "Sara, come on. Don't be scared. You know I would never hurt you. These people tried to hurt you. We need to leave, Sara, before they take you away from me again. I won't let them take you away from me again, Sara," he shouted, still holding out his hand to MacKenzie.

Tears started falling from MacKenzie's eyes, and she was shaking. "No, please, I'm not Sara. I'm MacKenzie," she cried. The man grabbed MacKenzie's arm and pulled her to him. MacKenzie screamed. That scream seemed to shake something in Davey to action. He pulled out his phone and sent an emergency text to Bear with the location.

The gunman spoke into MacKenzie's ear. "See, they have brainwashed you. I need to find a way to make you remember our life together. I will take you someplace safe and make you remember," he said, putting his arm around her neck while still pointing the gun at everyone. "Nobody better try and stop us or follow us. I might be forced to hurt Sara if you do. Don't make me do that," he said, pulling MacKenzie out the side door and down the stairs to the waiting car. The gunman put MacKenzie in the driver's seat and got in beside her, leveling the gun at her.

Davey ran after them and got the license plate number and the make and model of the car. Seconds later, sirens were heard, and police cruisers appeared from everywhere. Davey's phone was ringing. It was Bear.

"Bear, where are you?" Davey asked panicking.

"It's OK, buddy I'm on my way. I was visiting Bobby and Ty when I got your text. We're on our way," Bear said.

"Hurry, Bear, he has MacKenzie," Davey whispered.

Davey was sitting with the police captain when Bear and his brothers approached. "Whoa, there, this is official police business. You will all need to leave," the captain said.

Bear handed the captain the phone. "This is General O'Riley from the state department. That's his daughter who was taken, and he wants a word with you." He hugged Davey tight, and Bobby and Ty did the same. "We're going to get her back, Davey. My team will be here within the hour, and the General has given me authority over this situation with the police at my disposal." Bear saw the terror in Davey's eyes. "No harm will come to MacKenzie. I promise. You have my word, bro," he announced in a steely voice, gripping Davey's face. Davey looked into Bear's eyes and nodded.

When the captain ended the call, he looked at Bear. "You know some people in high places, my friend. This is now your investigation. Let me tell you what we know so far. Whatever you need from me and my department is yours for the asking," the captain said. "The gunman's name is George Smith. He's an on-again-off-again psychiatric patient. He lives with his elderly mother in the Bronx. I have some officers bringing her into the station. He seems to be fixated on MacKenzie O'Riley, thinking she is his fiancée, Sara Jones. Sara Jones died in a car accident with George several years ago. George suffered a brain injury and was never the same. Come with me to talk to his mother."

Bear nodded and turned to Davey. "My team will meet me at the police station. I need you and Bobby and Ty to go to the restaurant and stay there. Keep your phones on and charged in case MacKenzie calls. The restaurant can act as a base of sorts for our family. Call the rest of the family and let them know what's going on. But most importantly, Davey, I need you to let us do our job. Trust us. OK?" Bear said. Davey nodded and let Bobby and Ty lead him to his car.

Bear's team arrived at the station: Kate Wilder, sniper; Colt Jenness, electronics wizard; Mo Dawson, bomb specialist; and Travis James, computer specialist. In full combat attire, they were an impressive sight to behold. Bear and the police captain talked with the gunman's mother. George's elderly mother had suspected that her son was off his medication because of his ramblings about Sara. On Thursday, George had come home with the magazine with MacKenzie on the cover and told his mother that he had found Sara. He started obsessing about talking to her and asking why she left him. George's elderly mother had hoped that it would just pass; nevertheless, she had put in a call to George's counselor just that morning about her concerns for her son.

Bear asked George's mother if she knew where he might take MacKenzie. The only place that came to mind was a cabin in the woods in upstate New York. It was the cabin he and Sara were going to the day of the accident. George's mother had no idea where this cabin was, so the police captain sent officers to George's house to search for clues, and Bear and his team were contacting George's counselor to find out if he knew where this cabin was.

The police captain instructed his officers to go back in the database and find out what hospital had treated George and Sara and to get any police records from the accident. From what Bear had already learned about George, he knew that he was agitated and in a manic state. What concerned Bear was how George would react if he discovered MacKenzie was not his Sara. Bear scrubbed his hands over his face. They needed to find this cabin fast.

— ⁓

"A fucking Italian prince!" Davey said, staring at his computer. Davey sat at the bar of his restaurant with Bobby, Ty, Marcus, and Caleb. When they had gotten to the restaurant, Davey had grabbed his laptop and googled Roberto Savoy to find he was, in fact, a prince of the Italian royal family. What. The. Fuck? He had also scrolled through photos that the paparazzi posted from last year of the couple getting ice cream, kissing, and holding hands. Jesus. Davey punched the counter, waking Caleb who had his head down on the bar.

"Calm down, bro. What does it matter if he is the king of fucking England? She told you she loved *you*. Bear is going to bring her back, and you guys can straighten this shit out once and for all," Ty urged quietly.

Ty was right, he thought. If he ever got the chance to make it up to MacKenzie...well, he would spend his life trying to make up for being such an idiot. He was so terrified for her. He couldn't imagine even one day without seeing her beautiful face or hearing that raspy, sexy voice or her laugh. God, he loved her laugh. What if he never heard it again?

33

MacKenzie could feel herself starting to fall asleep. The gunman had insisted on her driving, and they had driven for hours. The adrenaline and fear had left her exhausted. The gunman had put on CDs of jazz music, playing them over and over. "I'm so tired. I think I'm going to fall asleep," MacKenzie pleaded, stealing a glance at the gunman.

"Don't worry, Sara, we're almost at the turnoff now," he replied, pointing to a dirt road that was hidden by overgrown trees.

MacKenzie turned off the highway and drove for several more miles before they came upon a small deserted cabin. "Do you remember the cabin, Sara?" the gunman asked when she turned off the car.

MacKenzie shook her head with eyes big. She said, "No, I'm sorry I don't."

The gunman smiled softly. "It's OK, Sara, it's late, and you're tired. We'll talk in the morning. Let's go inside."

He took her hand and led her up the rickety stairs to the cabin door. He held the gun in his other hand. "Open the door," the gunman said.

MacKenzie tried the door and found that it was ajar. She pushed open the door and heard something scurrying for cover. MacKenzie shivered to think what that "something" might be. The gunman had a flashlight and led MacKenzie to a back bedroom with an old cast-iron bed with just an old stained mattress. He nudged her forward to the bed.

MacKenzie started crying. "No, please, don't do this. Please," she pleaded.

"Shhh, hey, hey, it's OK. I'm not going to hurt you, Sara. Please don't cry. I just want you to lie down on the bed and get some rest. We will talk in the morning," the gunman replied. "I'm going to lie beside you," he said and draped an arm over her stomach.

MacKenzie lay on the smelly mattress as the gunman pulled her close to his chest. The tears silently fell onto the mattress as MacKenzie thought of Davey's smiling eyes and warm embrace. She said a silent prayer to heaven that if she ever got out of this, she would tell Davey how much she loved him and whatever time they might have together, she would cherish it.

It seemed like only minutes had passed when MacKenzie found herself being shaken awake violently.

"Sara, wake up! Come on, I need to show you something," the gunman exclaimed as he pulled her up off the bed, grasping her hand and roughly dragging her out of the cabin. It was still dark outside. MacKenzie tried to acclimate her eyes to the darkness. She was trying to stay on her feet rather than being dragged.

"Stop! Please stop! I'm going to fall!" MacKenzie pleaded.

The gunman didn't slow down but instead picked up the pace, and they began climbing the massive mountain surrounding the cabin.

MacKenzie tried with all her might to keep up, but after about a half hour of being pulled up the mountain, she tripped and cried out.

The gunman dragged MacKenzie a short way before stopping and kneeling down to face her. He was angry.

"Stop it, Sara! You know I've wanted to show you this for a long time. It's your own fault you made me come after you and scare you. You lied to me. You said you would never leave me. I've been searching for you forever. Now that I have you, I'm going to take you where we can be together alone. No more running away from me. Do you hear me?" he growled tugging on her hand to make his point.

MacKenzie cried out from how tight he was gripping her hand. She nodded.

"Yes...I won't run away. I promise. I'm so sorry, but I have forgotten your name. I don't know what's wrong with me," she said tearing up.

That seemed to diffuse the emotions in the gunman, because his grip softened and he looked at her with compassion.

"Oh, sweetheart, don't cry. I know what that's like. I forget things all the time. I'm George, your fiancé. Remember now?" he asked, gently touching her cheek.

MacKenzie sniffled and nodded.

"OK, good. Now, let's keep moving. We still have a long way to go," George said, gently helping MacKenzie up. He continued to climb and pull MacKenzie along, albeit at a slightly slower pace.

MacKenzie could tell he was manic and very emotionally unstable. It would be best to just go along with whatever he said so as not to upset or anger him. She was so tired and thirsty. She wondered dully how long a person could last without water.

34

It was almost dawn, and Bear and his team had the cabin surrounded, with police officers covering the roadways and the edges of the woods surrounding the cabin. The team had hit brick walls trying to find the cabin until a member of Bear's team, Travis, had found Sara's sister. They had her brought in for an interview, and she admitted she knew where the cabin was that her sister and George had been going to that day and gave the team directions to it. The General had arrived via helicopter. The same helicopter had dropped off the team a mile away from the cabin. The General stayed with the helicopter with a radio that monitored the team's transmissions.

There was no movement inside the cabin. Bear grabbed the bullhorn.

"George, this is Mason Johnson. I'm here to make sure nobody gets hurt. What I need from you, George, is for you to let me know that Sara is OK. Can you do that, George? I need for you to talk to me," Bear urged.

No response and no movement inside the cabin. That wasn't good. That sick feeling he got when shit started to go sideways was churning in his gut.

"George, in order for me to keep you safe, you need to talk to me. Let me know you and Sara are doing OK. Do you need anything? Can we bring you food or blankets? Talk to me, buddy," Bear said more insistently.

Silence. Shit. Bear motioned for his team to stand down as he stood in front of the cabin and lay his weapon on the ground at his feet. He raised his hands and slowly proceeded to the cabin door. His guts were churning. He didn't know what he was going to find inside that cabin. Hadn't he told Davey to trust him? Hadn't he promised him he would bring MacKenzie back to him safe and sound? Fuck.

Bear opened the front door and moved slowly inside the dilapidated structure. The sun was coming up, making it easier to see as he maneuvered around couches and chairs that had been left to rot. He checked everywhere except the back bedroom with the closed door. As he stood outside the door with his hand frozen inches from the doorknob, he said in a gentle voice, "George? I'm unarmed. I'm going to come in to check on you both, OK? I'm coming in now."

Bear slowly turned the knob, and with a loud creak, the door opened to an empty room. Bear took a deep breath, unaware he hadn't been breathing. Turning his head and speaking into the com on his shoulder, he let his team and the General know the subjects were not in the cabin and to reassemble in front of the cabin to reassess the situation.

It was so hot. MacKenzie was soaked with sweat. She was so thirsty she was light headed and listing as she walked hand in hand with George. They had been walking for hours. George seemed to know where he was going and kept urging her forward until he stopped and listened.

"Oh, we're almost there, Sara! Just a little farther. Can you hear that?"

Water. Lots of water. Mackenzie's throat closed up from thirst and hearing rushing water so close.

All of a sudden, the forest cleared into a scene from a fairytale. There was a small pond and stream that was fed by a gorgeous waterfall.

It was lush and green with moss covering everything and ferns thickly growing all around. Wow.

MacKenzie shook her hand free of George's and ran to the pond. Mouthful after mouthful she drank. Finally satisfied, she sat back to look around. George was still drinking but turned to see where she was.

He smiled. "It's beautiful, isn't it? This is why I wanted to bring you here so long ago. I knew you would love it as much as I do. I found it by mistake when I was hiking one day. You're the only girl I have ever wanted to bring here."

MacKenzie gave a wan smile. She was feeling a little better. "It is very beautiful here." Hesitating, she continued. "I will need to get back soon, George. I have to work tomorrow. You'll get me back in time for work, won't you, George?"

George scowled. "You're not going to trick me again, Sara! I won't let you leave me! You know I don't like it when you lie to me!" he said, getting in Mackenzie's face.

MacKenzie scooted back, afraid.

"Come on. I have something else to show you," he commanded, starting to wade into the pond.

MacKenzie tried to pull back. "Wait...What are you doing?" she asked, digging her heels into the soft soil.

"We're just going to swim over there," George said, pointing to the waterfall.

"George, I can't. I'm too tired to make it over there. I just don't have the strength," she whispered, sitting down.

"Sara, come on, you can do it. Just a little farther and you can rest. I'll help you," he insisted, pulling her into the water.

Panicking, MacKenzie resisted. "Wait...George, wait. Let me take my shoes off first. Please."

George released her hand, letting her pull her off her black flats and place them on the big rock beside the pond. If anybody came looking for them, hopefully these might lead them to her. MacKenzie grudgingly walked barefoot to the pond and took George's outstretched hand.

As the water quickly deepened, George let go of MacKenzie's hand to allow her to swim. They were about halfway to the waterfall when MacKenzie suddenly started to lose all strength and began to sink below the surface. She cried out just before her head sank below the surface. She felt herself floating downward but had nothing left in her to fight her way to the surface.

MacKenzie felt her arm yank upward, and she broke the surface with George's arm around her throat pulling her backward. Trying to cough and breathe, George plunged them both into the waterfall and MacKenzie into blackness.

35

Bear and his team had no problem tracking the pair. As there wasn't a trail to use, George had stumbled about, breaking fresh ground on his way up the mountain. Late that afternoon, the team tracked them to the water's edge and found MacKenzie's shoes. Good girl. They couldn't be far away because the tracks ended at the water. It was too risky to go any farther and risk making George feel desperate and cornered.

Bear had a gut feeling that they were behind the waterfall. The plan was to wait until morning or until they could separate George and MacKenzie. The team hunkered down at the edge of the forest and watched the pond. Bear walked into the woods and called the General to update him.

"Yes, sir. If Mac hadn't left her shoes on that rock, we wouldn't have known for sure that we were in the right vicinity. She's a smart cookie," Bear said with pride in his voice.

"That's my girl. I couldn't be more proud of her. If there is no sign of activity by dawn, I want your team to go in and get my daughter, Mason. Do whatever you have to do to achieve that objective. Do you understand that, Captain?"

Bear stiffened, hearing the all-out command in the General's voice. There would be no room for fuck-ups. None whatsoever.

"Sir, affirmative, sir." The line went dead. Bear took a deep breath, walked back to his team, and settled in for a night of watching the perimeter.

— ⁓

Just before dawn, with Bear and Kate stationed on either side of the waterfall, George appeared swimming under the waterfall. Mo and Colt were waiting just out of sight. George caught sight of Bear and began swimming back toward the waterfall. Bear dropped his gun and dove into the water, blocking George's entrance back under the waterfall. George began flailing around, trying to push past Bear.

"I won't let you take her away from me again!" George garbled, coughing and trying to breathe.

George was panicking and getting tired. Bear wasn't able to get a grip on him until he actually began slipping beneath the surface. Bear was then able to get behind George, place his arm under his chin, and pull him to the shore. Mo and Colt were there to take over and watch George as he lay on the mud trying to catch his breath.

Bear and Kate swam under the waterfall to a small alcove in the rocks. MacKenzie lay motionless away from the spray of water.

Bear gently picked up MacKenzie's head, stroking her cheeks with his thumbs.

"Wake up, Mac. It's me, Bear. You're safe now, sweetheart. Come on, wake up."

MacKenzie moaned and woke with a start, gasping in fear, her eyes wild and frightened.

Bear grasped her head looking steadily into her eyes. "Shhh, It's all right, Mac. You're safe now."

MacKenzie looked up, really seeing for the first time. Was she dreaming? No, it was Bear, and she was safe! MacKenzie started laughing and crying at the same time. Her whole body was shaking. "I was so scared, Bear," MacKenzie cried out, even as she started to calm down.

Bear held her close and kissed the top of her head. "I know. It's over now. You were very brave, sweetheart. You did good," Bear said. Through his earpiece, Bear spoke to his team. "You guys wait here with the target. I'm going to take baby bird and see her safely to papa bird. I'll be back with medical personnel to take care of the target. You did good, team. Me and my family appreciate it," Bear said, walking with MacKenzie out of the water and into the woods.

The cheering had died down and his brothers had gone home after hearing that MacKenzie was safe and on her way back to the police station. Davey had unashamedly cried in front of his brothers upon hearing the news. Davey had never been so frightened in his entire life. His only prayer had been for her safety. He had made so many deals with God throughout the night, involving everything from staying away from MacKenzie to making her his wife, but in the end, he had prayed that whatever the future held, his only wish was that MacKenzie made it home safe and unharmed. That wish had been granted. Thank God.

Davey heard the door open and figured one of his brothers had forgotten something. Davey looked up to see Roberto standing behind him. "It is good news, no?" Roberto said smiling.

Davey nodded. "Yes, it's very good news."

"I have come to ask a favor of you, Dave Johnson. Actually, a favor for MacKenzie," Roberto said.

Davey crossed his arms and narrowed his eyes. "Go on," he said.

Roberto put his hands in his pockets. "I plan to ask MacKenzie to come back to Italy with me and become my wife. A royal princess. The people of my country already love MacKenzie and think of her as their princess. I have the power to protect MacKenzie so nothing like this ever happens again. I assume you also want her safe? MacKenzie will want for nothing, and I will give her the children she so desires. I also have been sent here to offer her the position of head pastry chef of La Pergola. You see, Mr. Johnson, I alone have the capacity to make all MacKenzie's dreams come true. I know that you want MacKenzie to be happy, no? I'm asking you to stay away from her and let her make her own mind up. If she chooses to come back to Italy with me, then you will have her answer. Don't you owe her that much?" Roberto asked.

Davey felt like he'd been kicked in the gut. "I'm going to call her to make sure she's all right," Davey said angrily.

Roberto nodded. "Of course, but can you at least wait until she is settled at home? Give her some time with her father."

Davey felt like screaming, but he nodded. Roberto smiled and held out his hand.

"Get the fuck out," Davey said, turning back to the bar and pouring himself a scotch.

— —

"Roberto?" MacKenzie exclaimed, astonished, as the Italian walked into the police station where they were debriefing her.

Roberto ran to MacKenzie and embraced her. "Oh, *tesoro*, I am so happy you are safe. I have been so worried about you! Let me look at you, my amore," he said, kissing her face.

MacKenzie stepped away from Roberto. She looked around at the empty room. Her father and the officers must have thought she wanted privacy. Roberto motioned for her to sit down and knelt in front of her. "My *amore*, I came before the incident. I was at the competition to cheer you on. I'm afraid I have landed in a bit of trouble back home and need a friend. I need my very best friend in all the world," Roberto said, taking her hands in his.

"What do you need from me, Roberto?" MacKenzie said flatly.

"Well, you know how much my father respects you and your family. I feel that if you are with me when I confront my father, well, he will not deal with me quite so harshly," he said.

MacKenzie stood up and started pacing. "Roberto, you have to start cleaning up your own messes. You need to deal with your father on your own. It's not my concern any longer," she said, crossing her arms.

Roberto stood and nodded. "I know, *amore*. What I need most of all is a friend. I thought we were friends, MacKenzie. I thought you valued our friendship as much as I do," he said, leaning on the table with his head down.

MacKenzie's heart tugged. "Roberto, you know my friends are very, very important to me. But surely even you can see that it isn't the most convenient time for me. I was just taken hostage and had the fright of my life," she said imploringly.

Roberto stood and grasped her hands. "Oh, my *angelo*, it is the perfect time. You need to rest, and you can do that at the estate. You will be waited on hand and foot. You will want for nothing. I was also here on a mission to offer you the position as head pastry chef at La Pergola. You can come back to Italy with me and meet with Chef Verde and discuss your new position, yes?"

MacKenzie pulled her hands away and started pacing. She had her back to Roberto. "I met your boss, Dave Johnson. He thought it was a great opportunity for you," Roberto said softly.

MacKenzie's back stiffened, and she turned around slowly. "You met Davey?" MacKenzie asked.

Roberto nodded. "Yes, we waited at his restaurant for word of your safety.

MacKenzie nervously took a step closer. "Is that all he said?" MacKenzie asked.

"Yes, we didn't talk much. He seemed to be more concerned about drinking with his buddies at the bar. Please come back with me tonight, *tesoro*. Your father needs to be back in Washington for the peace talks, and I have the jet on standby. We can drop your father off on the way to Italy. Please, I really need a friend," Roberto pleaded.

MacKenzie's heart was heavy. Davey had met Roberto and gave his blessing for the job at La Pergola. Davey probably saw it as the perfect way out. No big scene with her when he officially ended their relationship.

She could just go quietly into the night where they both got what they wanted. She would get a prestigious position and a fresh start, and Davey would get off the hook after a no-strings-attached fling. At the very least, she did need time to get her head together and make some decisions about her life. She was done free-falling. It was time to decide what and who was important to her.

MacKenzie sighed sadly. "I would be happy to go back to Italy with you tonight. I need to go back to my apartment and get some clothes and hopefully see my friend Riley. Can you have your driver bring me to my apartment on the way to the airport?"

Roberto smiled and hugged her tightly. "Of course, *tesoro*," he said, ushering them to the waiting Bear and the police captain.

"Bear, am I all done here?" MacKenzie asked.

Bear smiled. "Yes, you can go get some rest now, sweetheart. You did great," he said, hugging her. Bear glared at Roberto as he ushered her out to the waiting car.

MacKenzie pulled her phone out of her bag that had been retrieved from the competition and dialed Davey. Davey picked up on the first ring.

"Baby, are you all right?" he asked urgently.

MacKenzie took a deep breath and then slowly exhaled. "Yes, I'm OK, thanks to Bear and his team. Davey, they were amazing. Listen, now that you're back at work, would you mind if I took this week off? I have some things to sort out, and a friend needs my help," she replied, looking at Roberto.

Davey's heart dropped. "Um, sure, of course. Take as much time as you need, MacKenzie. Will you let me know if there is anything I can do?" he asked quietly.

"This is something I need to do myself. There are some decisions I need to make. I will talk to you soon. Bye," she said and hung up.

MacKenzie asked Roberto to wait for her in the car as she gathered some things. When MacKenzie opened her apartment door, Riley screamed and ran to hug her. She was crying and almost hysterical.

"Hey, sweetie, calm down. I'm OK. It was terrifying, but everything turned out OK. Tell me, did you win the competition?" MacKenzie asked, leading her to the sofa.

Riley was shaking her head unbelievingly. "MacKenzie, you have just been taken hostage and you are curious about the *Cupcake Battles*?" she asked.

MacKenzie laughed. "I know, right? But yes, I want to know."

Riley smiled and blew her nose. "Yes, I did win, but I don't care about that. I am just so happy that you're OK," she exclaimed.

MacKenzie clapped her hands together. "Excellent. Now I have a favor to ask of you."

Riley nodded. "Anything."

"I am going to Italy tonight, but I will be back in one week. Will you stay in my apartment for me, and please not make any plans about your future? I mean it. In one week I will be back, and I will fill you in on the whole hostage thing, and we will talk about your future here in New York. Can you give me one week?" MacKenzie asked.

Riley narrowed her eyes. "What are you up to, MacKenzie O'Riley?" she asked.

MacKenzie touched the side of her nose. "I will reveal all in one week" was all she would offer as she started to throw clothes into her suitcase.

36

$\mathcal{I}$t had been two days since MacKenzie departed for Italy, and Davey felt himself sinking deeper and deeper down the rabbit hole. He drained his third glass of scotch of the evening and slumped back in his office chair. Suddenly, his office door flew open and all eight of his brothers, even Teddy, filed into his office.

"Hey, bro what's going on?" Bear asked, pushing Davey's feet off his desk. He picked up the bottle of scotch. "Oh, I see. A real mature way to deal with things for sure," Bear said sarcastically.

"Fuck off, all of you. I'm not drunk yet, but I'm well on my way, so if you don't mind, I'd like to be alone," Davey hissed, reaching for the bottle, which Bear kept in his hand as he walked to the couch.

Henry stood up to face Davey. "So let me get this straight. The lawyer in me really needs to get to the facts of this intriguing yet complex issue of love. You and MacKenzie love each other, but you let some smarmy Italian prince ride in here and whisk her away to Italy. Tell me, bro, what am I missing? Because the Mac we know and love would never have left without a good reason," Henry glowered, leaning on the desk in front of Davey.

"Well, I didn't exactly tell her how I felt about her, but I was going to. We were going to talk after the competition, but obviously we didn't get a chance," Davey retorted, pinching the bridge of his nose.

"OK, stay with me here. So you never actually told her how you feel. She wouldn't have been under the assumption that—oh, I don't know— you were never going to settle down and marriage and kids were out of the question, would she?" Henry practically shouted, not mincing any words.

Davey winced and remained silent.

"Oh, for fuck's sake, Davey. I knew it!" Bobby exploded, pacing the room.

Davey stood up and leaned on his desk. "I didn't plan on falling in love with her. It just happened. Then when it did, it scared the shit out of me, so I tried to tell myself that we could still just ride it out until we fell out of love. But I know now that that is never going to happen. Actually, I realized that before we ever left Moose Pond, and that's what I was going to tell her after the competition, but I never got the chance." He sat back down hard in his chair.

Apparently, it was now Teddy's turn to bitch slap Davey because he stood up. "So, that's it? You're just going to get drunk and wallow in your own stupendous fuck-up? Well, it doesn't take a rocket scientist, which I am, and by the way, I have waited my entire life to use that phrase, to see that you need to get off your ass and try to make this right, or you're going to regret it the rest of your life."

When Teddy said "regret it the rest of your life" with extreme emphasis, Davey suddenly remembered his mother telling him just that in his dream. Jesus. Fuck. His brothers were right; he needed to try and make this right. Davey sat bolt upright. "What do I do?" he asked his brothers.

Teddy crossed his arms over his chest. "Well, according to Bear, you must woo her, whatever the fuck that means."

Bear pointed to Teddy. "Yeah, you and me later, bro," he smirked.

Davey looked terrified. "I'm scared. What if she rejects me?"

Jared stood up and put his hands in his pockets. "That's what love is, Davey. Putting your whole self out there. Baring your soul to the one you love beyond anything else in the world. If you have the courage to do that, then I promise you, it will be worth it."

Bear laughed and grabbed Jared around the neck. "Says the man who took old Bear's advice and is engaged right this very minute to our very own princess!" Bear exclaimed proudly.

"Bear's right, Davey. You need to go fight for MacKenzie," Ty said.

"Yeah, are you going to let some Italian soccer-playing Casanova steal Mac away from you? I mean, if you don't go and get her back I will," Caleb said.

Davey started toward Caleb with murder in his eyes.

"Ah, not helping, Caleb," Garrett responded dryly.

Davey grabbed his head, trying to think. "I need to book a flight and pack a bag."

"Done and done," Henry said.

"What?" Davey stammered.

"The company jet is on standby waiting for you at the airport, and your suitcase is packed and in the car that's waiting out front to take you to the airport. Mike has been notified and told that there would be a big bonus in this for making him take charge yet again. Now get the hell out of here and go get our girl back," Henry barked.

"Oh, and, bro, I love how you fold all your underwear," Bobby smirked, and they all chuckled.

"Frig you guys, you can live like pigs if you want to, but I have some class," Davey retorted, but with a small smile for the first time in a while. He jumped up, and his brothers cleared the way for him to hustle out of the restaurant and hop into the waiting town car.

"Best brothers ever! Love you guys!" Davey hollered over his shoulder. Fucking-A-Skippy, he was going to bring his girl home, and if his prayers were answered, he would make her his bride, and soon they would have all kinds of little redheads running around the restaurant!

37

"So let me get this straight. You are not in any trouble. You just told me that to get me to come to Italy with you? It's all a lie?" MacKenzie asked, disgusted, her voice rising as she continued. They were in the limo leaving the Italian airport before Roberto had finally admitted that he wasn't in trouble and they didn't need to confront his father.

Roberto looked panicked. "No! It's not all a lie, *tesoro*," he said.

"Oh, don't *darling* me!" MacKenzie snarled with fire in her eyes.

"I admit that I did appeal to your fierce love and loyalty to your friends to get you to come to Italy, but I was desperate, *amore*! I do love you, and I do wish for you to be my bride. You are beloved by all Italy! And the position as head pastry chef at La Pergola is legitimate, my *angelo*. Chef Verde himself beseeched me to beg you to come back, *amore*," Roberto whined in a rather singsong voice.

MacKenzie rolled her eyes and picked up Roberto's hand. "Roberto, you are my oldest and dearest friend. You're right; I do love and protect my friends. I will never take my friendships for granted. But with that said, Roberto, that is how I think of you. I love you like a brother. I tried to convince myself that it was more than that when I tried to let you sweep me off my feet, but really, if I'm honest with myself, when I found you cheating, I was more upset that I had lost a dear friend. I think I was actually relieved not to have to make the decision to break off our relationship. As far as the head pastry chef job is concerned, I am very happy in New York. I love my job and the life that I have built," she said softly.

Roberto picked her hand up and held it to his lips. "That is not all you love in New York, is it, *amore*?" he asked, looking MacKenzie in the eyes.

MacKenzie teared up and shook her head. "See, you know me too well. I do love Davey with all my heart, and I am going to tell him so when I get home. Now bring me to a hotel, and I will go to La Pergola and see Chef Verde tomorrow, and then you can fly me home, you scoundrel," she replied, playfully punching his arm, the anger gone.

Roberto put his arm around her shoulders and laid his head beside hers. "He is a truly lucky man, *tesoro*," he said with a sigh.

39

avey flew all night and hired a car to take him straight to La Pergola. He figured he had a better chance of getting into the restaurant than a castle or whatever the fuck the royal family lived in. He wouldn't stand a chance of getting to her if he was in an Italian prison. As soon as the car stopped in front of the restaurant, Davey threw a handful of money at the driver, told him to wait, jumped out of the car, and ran inside. The hostess saw the panicked expression on his face; he was speaking loudly in Italian and using lots of hand gestures. "*MacKenzie Rose O'Riley*," he kept repeating to a blank face.

Eventually, another server recognized MacKenzie's name and pointed to the kitchen area. Davey started toward the kitchen, but the hostess put her hand on his chest and shook her head. Davey picked up her hand and kissed it. "I'm so sorry, sweetie, but you are not keeping from that kitchen," he said and darted around her. He burst through the doors to find MacKenzie speaking perfect Italian to a dozen fresh-faced pastry chefs, who were listening to every word out of her mouth intently. Jesus, she spoke fluent Italian. Of course she did. God, he loved her!

"MacKenzie, am I too late?" Davey asked breathlessly.

MacKenzie jumped back. "Davey? What are you doing here?"

Davey grasped her by the shoulders. "Sweetheart, please tell me, am I too late? Are you engaged?" Davey asked urgently. "Because if you are, you can just tell that bastard that I am going to fight for you. You're mine, MacKenzie Rose, and I won't let you leave me!" he exclaimed with heat.

MacKenzie gasped and looked around at everyone holding their breath waiting for her answer. She took Davey's hand, led him to a back pantry, and closed the door. Davey grasped MacKenzie's face, gently pushed her against the door, took her lips urgently. He put all the love and intensity he had in him into that kiss. He tasted her and nibbled her until neither of them could breathe. "Tell me I'm not too late, MacKenzie," Davey whispered.

MacKenzie moaned and smiled. "No, you're not too late. Roberto admitted that he got me here deceitfully by telling me he was in trouble and needed me to help him confront his father. Once he came clean, he did propose, but I declined. I told him my heart belonged to another." She was barely able to finish the thought before Davey was kissing her again and hiking her legs around his waist so she was directly rubbing against his erection.

Davey moaned. "Baby, I love you. That's what I was going to tell you after the competition. Speaking of which, I knew you threw the competition the minute I saw your choice of cupcake," he said between kisses.

"Wait. You were at the competition?" MacKenzie replied, surprised.

"Of course I was there, sweetheart. I love you, and I wanted to tell you that after you finished. That's where I first saw Roberto. He told me he was going to propose to you and make you a princess and about this job offer. He said he was going to make all your dreams come true. When we knew you were safe, he came to the restaurant and asked me to stay away from you. He said he could protect you. I can't protect you like that, sweetheart," Davey said, leaning his forehead against hers.

MacKenzie smiled. "Oh, Davey, Roberto can't make all my dreams come true. Only you can and you have. You love me!"

"Oh, baby, so much! I know I am fucking this all up, but will you marry me?" Davey asked, looking into her eyes.

"Davey, I thought you were totally against marriage," MacKenzie replied suspiciously.

Davey looked askance. "Oh, don't remind me of what an ass I've been. Can you forgive me?"

MacKenzie beamed. "There's nothing to forgive, my love. I will let you spend the rest of our lives making it up to me."

Davey laughed. "So, that's a yes?"

"Yes! Yes! Yes!" she said, laughing.

Davey hugged her and let her slide slowly to a standing position. "Can we get away from here, somewhere private? I really need you all to myself."

MacKenzie smiled and took his hand. They ran through the kitchen, hearing cheers behind them, then through the dining room and into the still-waiting car. As they collapsed into the back seat, tangled in each other's arms, MacKenzie gave her hotel address to the driver in Italian.

Davey put the Do Not Disturb sign on the handle of the door and shut and locked it. He took his cell phone, held his hand out for MacKenzie's, and turned them both off. They looked each other in the eyes and smiled. "Finally," Davey said, pulling MacKenzie into his arms. He gently traced the sides of her face. Tears gathered behind his eyes. "MacKenzie, I love you so much. I was so afraid to open up. I'm still afraid, terrified actually, of losing you like my father lost my mother, but not being with you hurts more than my fear. Thank you for being so strong and loving me even when I was being a shit." He kissed her gently.

MacKenzie smiled brightly. "Davey, it's always been you. I've loved you for as long as I can remember, but I still find myself falling deeper in love with you each day. How is that possible? How can a love be that big?"

Davey kissed her, deeply tasting her and claiming her with his mouth. MacKenzie tasted right back, letting her tongue invade his mouth deeply. Davey moaned and caught his breath. "Jesus," he whispered as he let his lips travel down her neck to nip and kiss. He unbuttoned her white blouse slowly, letting it fall to the floor, and unfastened her bra, letting that, too, fall to the floor. He slowly kissed down to the waiting breast, her nipples peaked and ready. He slowly let his mouth take in her full nipple and suck gently.

MacKenzie moaned loudly and bowed her back. "Davey," she said breathlessly.

Davey slowly lifted his head and blew softly on her peaked nipple. "What, baby? What do you need. Tell me," he said, continuing to blow gently.

MacKenzie inhaled a deep breath. "You. I need you, Davey. Please," she begged.

"Shhh. You have me, baby. You've bewitched me, body and soul," he said, unbuttoning her slacks and letting them fall to the floor. He knelt before her and pulled her panties down, and she stepped out of them. He picked her up and laid her down on the bed. God, what a sight to behold. She looked like a glorious angel with flame hair spread out on the white pillow.

MacKenzie looked beseechingly at him. "Hurry, Davey," she whispered.

Davey unbuttoned his shirt with shaky hands. Fumbling, he discarded his slacks and boxers and socks in a heap on the floor.

MacKenzie watched him intently. "So beautiful," she said as Davey's body covered hers.

The moment their skin touched, Davey moaned and took her mouth. MacKenzie couldn't keep her hands on one spot on his body; she wanted to touch him everywhere. She still couldn't believe he was here. He had flown halfway around the world to make sure she didn't marry another man. As if! MacKenzie stroked his back and hair and then moved her hands down to his perfect bum. She kneaded and pressed him against her core.

Davey grunted and moaned. "Oh, baby, we need to slow down, or I'm not going to last. I want you so badly I can hardly stand it," he said, dipping down and taking her breast into his mouth and sucking.

MacKenzie arched her back as a slow moan fell from her parted lips. Davey edged lower, kissing and nibbling until he reached her sex, nuzzling the soft red hair at her apex. He gently grasped her thighs and spread them wide apart, completely exposing her. He looked up and met her desire-filled eyes and parted lips. "Jesus, MacKenzie, you're beautiful," he whispered.

She smiled as he lowered his head to taste her. Her smile quickly turned into a gasp as he began to lick and taste her in earnest. Davey had to keep a hand on her abdomen to keep her on the bed. MacKenzie writhed and moaned and screamed as Davey inserted two fingers into her and continued to lick and suck. She was close, so close to completely falling apart that when Davey found her clit and began to suck gently, she broke into a million pieces, screaming his name and clutching his hair in her hands. He kissed her thighs gently as she stopped spasming and started sighing contentedly.

Davey crawled up her body until they were face to face. MacKenzie kissed him, tasting herself. "Baby, are you ready for me because I need to be inside you badly," he said as if in pain.

MacKenzie reached down and guided him into her. Davey moaned and buried himself in one stroke inside her. "You're mine, MacKenzie. Do you hear me? Mine," he said, driving into her.

MacKenzie could feel the stirring deep in her belly. Davey stopped, buried deep inside her, and kissed her. MacKenzie moaned. "Oh, Davey, don't stop, please," she begged.

Davey clutched MacKenzie's face and looked at her with tears in his eyes. "I'm so sorry if I hurt you, sweetheart. I was so scared you would be hurt or taken from me. I couldn't stand that, MacKenzie," he said as a tear fell onto her cheek.

"Hey, hey, I'm not going anywhere, and I wasn't hurt. I just kept thinking of your smiling eyes, and I knew I had to make it back to you. I love you," she said with tears in her own eyes.

"Never leave me again, MacKenzie. Promise me," Davey demanded as he began to move in and out of her again.

"I promise," MacKenzie whispered as she felt herself begin to lift higher and higher. Davey hollered MacKenzie's name as he came apart as never before. MacKenzie was right there with him as she, too, came in a spectacular display of complete loss of control and cried Davey's name over and over.

Completely sated, MacKenzie lay on top of Davey with her hand under her chin, grinning. Davey grinned back with his hands behind his head, feeling like the king of the world. "So, you're completely sure about marrying a simple restaurateur instead of becoming an Italian princess?"

MacKenzie laughed, a sound he would never get sick of. "I am disgustingly happy," she said contentedly.

"Good, because you will always be my queen," Davey said, lifting up to kiss her. "I was thinking that when we get back home, you would move in with me until the wedding. I know the General won't really like that, but there is a logic to my thinking, so hear me out. If you move in with me, Riley could take over your apartment and continue to run Sweet Love," he said.

MacKenzie's eyes got big, and she smiled.

"Oh, I'm not done, sweetheart. I know Charlotte is going to give birth any day now, and she is looking to sell the shop. I was thinking that maybe you and I could be silent investors with Riley. She could pay us back and then completely take over. Kind of what Dad did with Jared. Look how well that turned out," Davey said, smiling.

Tears formed in MacKenzie's eyes. "Oh, Davey, you would do that?" she whispered.

Davey gently grasped her face. "*We* will do that. MacKenzie, I'm not sure you understand how much I love you and that there isn't anything I wouldn't do for you. I know how important your friends are to you, and now they're my friends, too," he said, kissing her.

MacKenzie rolled off Davey and onto her side facing him. "I think you underestimate the General. He's not as prudish as people think. True, he was very strict when I was growing up, but all he really wants is for me to be happy. He knows how much I love you and how happy you make me. As a matter of fact, I think he was rooting for you all along. I seem to remember him referring to Roberto as a pansy ass."

Davey laughed out loud. "I always liked the General, and so did my dad. "Speaking of parents," he said, "how long are you going to make me wait to marry you, sweetheart?"

MacKenzie looked at him dreamily. "Um, is fall too soon?"

Davey pretended that he was thinking. "Two months? I think that's doable, but I would marry you today if it was possible," he said, rolling over on top of her, letting her feel his constant reaction to her.

MacKenzie grasped his hair in her hands and pulled his head to her for a kiss.

"Oh, and one more thing, sweetheart. Eventually, we are going to have several little red-haired kids running around our restaurant," Davey said, capturing her lips in a deep kiss.

MacKenzie sighed. Could you die of happiness? she thought.

40

On a beautiful warm September day in Harmony, Maine, MacKenzie stood in the giant tent set up in the park. Brenna O'Riley stood looking at her beautiful daughter, dressed in full Scottish wedding attire made specifically for MacKenzie by Brock Worthington. Brenna's ancestors would be proud indeed to see her MacKenzie in all her splendor.

The dress. MacKenzie sighed, looking at her mother in the mirror as they admired the dress. It was yards of white silk in a medieval off-the-shoulder style with puffy cap sleeves that continued from the shoulder to hug the length of her arms. There was embroidery stitching in a green Celtic design on the cap sleeves. The rest of the dress fit her body like a glove with no adornments, just smooth white satin. Draped low on her hips was a large scarf of green tartan that gathered in the back with the white silk train. The green tartan came from her direct ancestors' clan. MacKenzie wore white silk ballet flats on her feet. Her flame-red hair had been gathered in a knot with tendrils falling around her face. Her mother placed little white flowers in her hair and fastened a string of perfect white pearls around her neck. A gift from her and the General.

The music started and Jack ran over to her from where she had been embracing her brothers. All except Davey, who was waiting outside the tent for Jack and his brothers to come out. Jack had tears in her eyes. "Can you believe it, Macadoo? We're getting married! This is the happiest day of my entire life, and I'm so glad I get to share it with you. Now we really will be sisters."

MacKenzie laughed and embraced Jack. "I always wanted a best friend, but never in my wildest dreams did I ever think I would have a sister and best friend."

Marcus came to take Jack's hand. "I'll see you at the gazebo!" Jack ended, running out of the tent and back to her brothers.

Brenna grasped MacKenzie's face gently. "Your dad and I are so proud of you, MacKenzie. What a strong, lovely lass you have grown up to be."

MacKenzie welled up. "Oh, Momma, I'm so happy!" she whispered.

"That's all we've ever wanted for you, love," her mother replied, hugging her.

The General walked into the tent and stared at his two beautiful Scottish lasses. He cleared his throat. "You must be getting to your seat there, Mrs. O'Riley. Our daughter is about to be married, don't ya know?" he said with a grin and a wink. Brenna smiled at her handsome husband in full military regalia.

"Oh, aye, you don't think I know what's about to happen, you old Irish fool," Brenna said, kissing her husband and walking out of the tent.

The General smiled after his wife with love shining in his eyes. He grasped MacKenzie's hands. "Oh, your mother will have already told you how proud we are of you, so I won't go on about it. But know this, my baby girl. I still remember the day you were born, screaming to high heaven with your thatch of red hair and big curious blue eyes and perfect fingers and toes. I've gotten medals for valor and bravery and been proud of them, but nothing, and I mean nothing, compares to how proud I was the day you were born and the pride I feel as I look upon you today. You have always had my heart, and you always will be my MacKenzie Rose," he proclaimed, linking her arm with his and walking toward the entrance to the tent.

As they exited the tent into the beautiful sunshine, MacKenzie looked out at all her friends and family and felt so blessed. Her eyes found Davey, standing at the gazebo with his brothers and Jack and Jared.

Davey had never seen MacKenzie look more beautiful than she did right then, wearing her Scottish wedding dress with her clan tartan. She took his breath away. He hoped his mother and father were here with them right now. He knew how happy they would be that he had taken their advice and had not wasted the love that he and MacKenzie had for each other. He smiled through the tears as the General handed him his very heart and agreed to let Davey love her the rest of his days, which came as easily as breathing and was just as necessary.

Epilogue

"Oh, Jesus, this one's a strong one!" Davey said, looking at the monitor reading MacKenzie's contractions. He looked up instantly, regretting opening his mouth as MacKenzie looked at him with excruciating pain on her face. "Oh God, I'm sorry, baby. OK, now, look at me. Just like in class. Breathe out with me, one, two, three. Now again he, he, he," Davey said over and over.

MacKenzie moaned loudly. "I feel like I need to push!" she cried.

Davey took the cloth and wiped her face. "It's not time, baby. Just a little while longer, I promise. You're doing so great!"

"Did my parents' plane get in yet?" MacKenzie gasped as another contraction took over, and she practiced the breathing technique she and Davey had learned in Lamaze class.

"They're not here yet, sweetie, but there's a military helicopter on its way. It will be landing on the roof of the hospital shortly." Davey smiled and tried to breathe with MacKenzie. He was pretty sure he wouldn't be able to use his hands for days because MacKenzie was gripping them so tightly. She was so much stronger than he'd given her credit for. "But you will be happy to know that the waiting room is so full of our family and friends that I'm afraid we're over hospital capacity," he said, smiling, knowing all his brothers and Jack and Jared were waiting not so patiently for the birth of the first two baby Johnsons.

Davey still remembered the day MacKenzie had whispered in his ear after making love that they were pregnant. The instant love and gratitude he had felt spilled over and had them both laughing and crying until they fell asleep in each other's arms. They had taken a year after they were married to travel all over the world when they weren't working like dogs at the restaurant. For a wedding present, Davey had presented MacKenzie with a new deed to the restaurant with both their names on it. They were truly partners in every aspect of their lives.

MacKenzie cried out in pain. "Davey, distract me, please. I need to push," she pleaded as the contraction subsided.

Davey took her hand, brought it to his lips, and looked her in the eyes. "Would you like to know when I knew I was in love with you?" he asked.

MacKenzie gave a tired smile and nodded.

"It was when you told me about your childhood dinnertime ritual of telling five things that amazed or interested you or that you had loved about that day. I remember thinking how wonderful it was to look at the world around you with such awe. That night, I listed five good things about my day. Do you know what was at the top of my list?"

MacKenzie shook her head, feeling a really big contraction coming.

"You. You were at the top of that list, and every day since then and for the rest of my life, you will always be at the top of my list because you amaze me and interest me, and I love you more than I ever thought possible," he answered softly as MacKenzie's hand tightened painfully around his own.

A single tear slipped down MacKenzie's cheek as she whispered, "I love you," and screamed as the urge to push took over.

— —

MacKenzie gazed down at her son with the dark hair and dark eyes, sleeping soundly. "David Edwin Johnson Jr. has a lovely ring to it," she said, smiling over at Davey who was lying beside her on the hospital bed, holding their daughter, Brenna Elsie Johnson. Davey couldn't take his eyes off her. She had a head full of flame-red hair and blue eyes and the tiniest fingers and toes he had ever seen. He couldn't even begin to describe the intense love he'd felt the moment he set eyes on his son and daughter. The family had all taken turns coming in and meeting the newest and most eagerly anticipated additions to the family. Even Jack had been allowed to come to the hospital, albeit in a wheelchair. She was on total bedrest until her babies were born in one month.

MacKenzie dusted her hand gently over baby Brenna's soft hair and leaned her head on Davey's shoulder. "All my life, I always believed that I would fall in love, and we would make a home and life in one place. No more moving from country to country or state to state. I would finally have a forever home. Now I know that you're my home—my world. It doesn't matter where we are. As long as we're together, I'm home."

Preview of Heaven, Book 3

*M*arcus watched as a cab pulled up to the curb in front of his club, Heaven, and a beautiful white-blond-and-pink-haired woman stepped out of the cab in a white cocktail dress and killer high heels, followed by a punk rocker woman with black spikey hair in jeans and thigh-high boots. He continued to watch as a pair of strappy black heels with diamond studded toes emerged, then black leather pants and a leather jacket. As the third woman stepped out of the car, Marcus could see a full head of red curls. *Mac.* Marcus smiled as he watched Davey, his younger brother, standing on the curb completely dumbstruck and then marching over to Mac.

Marcus knew there was something between his brother and his sister's best friend. It looked as if they were having a difficult time navigating their feelings for each other, but it was best to not get involved. As the oldest of ten siblings, Marcus had found out the hard way that what he thought was best wasn't necessarily the right decision.

Marcus's eyes traveled back to the blond-and-pink-haired woman. She was exquisite, like a fairy princess or an angel from above. She was petite with the sexiest pair of legs he had ever seen in sky-high stilettos that made her slight stature less obvious. The white cocktail dress was flowy with a little pink belt around her waist that accented her voluptuous breasts. His hungry eyes continued higher to her crowning glory, a mass of white-blond-and-pink hair that flowed over her shoulders down to her derriere. Marcus was slightly frustrated that he couldn't quite make out her facial features from the second-story window. From where he stood, the woman looked like a virginal sacrifice on her way to the arena to be eaten by hungry lions, which wasn't altogether untrue considering the nature of the club she was about to enter.

Marcus could feel his pulse quicken, and a light sheen of sweat covered his brow as he watched the blonde and the rocker chick walk toward the long line that had formed outside the club. He picked up his walkie-talkie to alert the doorman to let the women proceed ahead of the line directly into the club. He watched the screen as the laughing women entered the large bar area. Heads turned to look the newcomers over with interest. Lions indeed. The women made their way to the bar and sat down. Marcus spoke to the bartender through his walkie-talkie, instructing him to give the two women whatever they asked for on the house. The bartender poured a beer for the rocker chic, and Marcus watched him hesitate before nodding and bending down to retrieve a bottle from the collection of exclusive whiskeys. The bartender pulled out a bottle of Johnnie Walker Blue, and Marcus smiled. The blonde had exceptional taste.

Marcus watched as the rocker chick surveyed the crowd and blended in comfortably. The blonde, on the other hand, never took her eyes off her drink or her friend. Never once looked around. Clearly, this was her first time in an S&M club. She looked about to bolt at any second. He was enthralled as he regarded her downcast eyes carefully and saw that after each sip of whiskey, she would caress her lower lip with her tongue as if she was trying to savor each swallow of the decadent liquor. Uncomfortable. Marcus was barely able to sit still; he was so aroused by her body language and that sweet pink tongue. Jesus, he couldn't remember a time when he had been so intrigued or, truthfully, when his cock had been this hard. All without ever speaking to the blond bombshell or even being in her immediate vicinity.

Brushing his fist back and forth over his mouth, Marcus jumped up, headed for the elevator, and pressed the button for the main floor.

◦— —◦

Zena sat ramrod straight, feeling eyes boring into her back. Attention didn't bother Zena even though, for as long as she could remember, she had tried with all her might to blend into the woodwork. If you weren't any trouble, then maybe the foster family would consider keeping you. Most times, it didn't matter because all she amounted to was a paycheck for them. There might have been great foster families out there, but Zena had not been fortunate enough to find one. As soon as she had developed boobs, she was either groped by the males in the house, or the wife would ship her out the door the first chance she got, considering Zena a threat. The only person Zena had ever been able to count on was Trina, whom she had met in the Goodwill Children's Home. Goodwill was a last stop for kids who weren't wanted in foster care either because they were troublemakers or because they were too old to be considered for adoption. Zena had lived there from age fourteen to eighteen with Trina, her best friend and sister by choice.

Trina had left to dance when Zena felt the presence of someone beside her at the bar. He leaned in and with hot breath said into her ear, "I've not seen you here, lass. What are ye drinking?"

The thick Scottish accent caressed her senses. Almost enough to get her to look at him, but not quite. Zena lifted her glass and took a slow sip. "Johnnie Walker Blue," she said, setting her drink back on the bar. Waiting for a response with her head down, she suddenly felt the energy change dramatically and sizzle with something she couldn't quite name. Then a deep, sultry, purely American voice echoed in her ear.

"You know you're torturing every male and a good number of the females in this club right now."

Zena drew a sharp breath. This voice didn't caress at all. It sizzled through her entire nervous system, ending in her nether regions and making her head snap up to look at the mysterious stranger. The intensity of his gaze made Zena forget to breathe for a moment or two. She was staring into the most intense glacier-blue eyes she had ever seen. He had features that were chiseled out of granite, which gave him a stern brow. His hair was dark brown and closely cropped. It looked as if he had run his hands through it in frustration multiple times, giving him a rough look. Adding to that was a two-day beard growth that had Zena wondering what the rough beard would feel like on the insides of her thighs.

What? Wait! Zena blinked, trying to get the ground back under her. She picked up her drink with a slightly shaking hand and took a sip. As she set the drink back on the bar, she turned to him again. "What about you? Am I torturing you?" she asked in a breathy voice. Zena thought for sure he could hear her heart beating; it was so loud in her own ears.

The stranger motioned to the bartender, who seemed to be waiting for a command from him. The bartender immediately refilled Zena's drink and poured two fingers of Johnny Walker Blue for the stranger. "Will there be anything else, master?" the bartender inquired.

Zena's eyes got wide, and she looked from the bartender to the stranger with her mouth open and her big, blue eyes holding his stare. Without taking his eyes off Zena, he gave a barely noticeable tilt to his head, and the bartender quickly headed to the center of the bar away from them. "It seems that I am in a bit of a dilemma. If I say no, you will think I'm not interested, which would be a bold-faced lie. But if I say yes, and honestly tell you that I can scarcely remember a time I was this intrigued or aroused and that I would almost sell my soul right this very minute to be able to bend you over and spank that perfect ass and fuck you so hard that you would remember this night for as long as you live, I fear that you will run for the hills. Which is what you should do, I might add," he said, leaning into her.

Zena didn't think it was possible for her eyes to get any wider, as they were already practically up to her hairline, but she looked at him barely able to breathe and licked her lips nervously. The stranger groaned and downed his whiskey in one gulp. The bartender was there refilling his glass immediately.

The stranger took a sip and looked over at her. "You're killing me here," he said with a slight smirk.

Zena shook her head and took a sip from her glass, keeping her eyes on it as she set it back on the bar. "I don't scare easily. I have to admit that I usually don't shock easily either, but you did catch me off guard, I suppose. I think I half expected to be dragged to a dungeon and chained to a wall. So yes, I'm a little on edge. Your blunt honesty is a refreshing change," she said, looking back up at him. He was still leaning sideways with his right arm resting on the bar and looking directly at her. The electricity between them was almost unbearable for Zena. He smiled, and his whole face changed from an intense warrior to the sexiest man alive in a heartbeat. She just stared, transfixed.

"I would never chain you up without your consent, angel, and my bedroom has been called many things, but never a dungeon, I can assure you," he said, leaning so close to her she could feel his warm breath on her cheek.

It was Zena's turn to silently moan with lust. She had never been so turned on by just talking to a man, and you could hardly call this talking. With her heart beating out of her chest, she decided to take this a little further. After all, wasn't that why she had let Trina talk her into coming here tonight? She was tired of just existing and constantly hiding behind her business and a few friends. It was time she stopped hiding in the shadows.

"I'm afraid you have approached the wrong sex partner tonight. I'm pretty vanilla, I'm sorry to say. I know nothing about this lifestyle, and I'm not sure I want to. I can tell you are either the owner of this club or a boss, the way everybody is waiting to do your bidding. I'm quite sure you can have anybody in this club, so I'll let you rethink your decision to approach me and thank you for the drinks. I think I'll call it a night," Zena said, turning in her seat to lower herself to the floor.

The stranger caught her arm in a firm grip and looked deeply into her blue eyes. "I'm not mistaken at all. Everyone is surprised to see me on the floor because I never come down here, but when I saw you on the monitor in my office, I couldn't contain my need to see if you were real. I would like you to come upstairs with me. I can promise you will not be harmed in any way, and we will stop anything you're not comfortable with immediately. I can also promise you that you are about as far away from vanilla as you can get." His lips were inches from her own. "There is one more thing. You must follow my instructions completely. You must submit to me. Can you do that, angel?" he asked.

Zena's head was spinning, and she could hardly breathe. Could she? She had fought so hard for complete control of every aspect of her life, and it was choking the life out of her. Maybe she could see what it would be like to submit willingly to another for one night. Let someone else make the decisions for her pleasure. Mind made up, she smiled brightly, taking his breath away.

"Lead the way."

About the Author

Maine resident Holly J. Martin has always had a passion for literature. Her beautiful home state is one of many inspirations for her series of romance novels, which follows the lives of the Johnsons. Martin, her husband, and their two cats live in central Maine.